True to You

TONY CORREIA

JAMES LORIMER & COMPANY LTD., PUBLISHERS
TORONTO

James Lorimer & Company Ltd., Publishers acknowledges the support of
the Ontario Arts Council (OAC), an agency of the Government of Ontario,
which in 2015-16 funded 1,676 individual artists and 1,125 organizations in
209 communities across Ontario for a total of $50.5 million. We acknowledge
the support of the Canada Council for the Arts, which last year invested $153
million to bring the arts to Canadians throughout the country. This project
has been made possible in part by the Government of Canada and with the
support of the Ontario Media Development Corporation.

Cover design: Shabnam Safari
Cover image: Shutterstock

Library and Archives Canada Cataloguing in Publication

Correia, Tony, author
       True to you / Tony Correia.

"Real love."
Issued in print and electronic formats.
ISBN 978-1-4594-1255-2 (softcover).--ISBN 978-1-4594-1256-9 (EPUB)

       I. Title.

PS8605.O769T78 2017   jC813'.6   C2017-903313-1
                                               C2017-903314-X

Published by:	Distributed in Canada by:	Distributed in the US by:
James Lorimer &	Formac Lorimer Books	Lerner Publisher Services
Company Ltd., Publishers	5502 Atlantic Street	1251 Washington Ave. N.
117 Peter Street, Suite 304	Halifax, NS, Canada	Minneapolis, MN, USA
Toronto, ON, Canada	B3H 1G4	55401
M5V 0M3		www.lernerbooks.com
www.lorimer.ca		

Manufactured by Friesens Corporation in Altona, Manitoba,
Canada in July 2017.
Job #234940

For Mette Bach.

Thanks for helping me rebuild Tara.

01 Principal's Office

AS I WAIT OUTSIDE Principal Shadrach's door, I'm staring at the bandages on my hands. This is the third time I've been here in as many months. Dad enters the office, out of breath and wearing his apron from the shop.

"I'm looking for Jorge Gomez," he says to the secretary. He pronounces it like *George* but the G sound is softer.

The secretary gestures in my direction. Dad grabs

me by the shoulders. He looks me up and down for signs I am hurt.

"What happened to your cheek?" he says.

"It's nothing." I look away.

"You look like you got hit by a truck!"

Principal Shadrach pokes his head out of the door. "Mr. Gomez? Jorge? I'm ready to see you." Mr. Shadrach offers Dad and I a seat. "I'm afraid Jorge got into another fight today."

"What happened this time?" Dad asks.

"It seems Ian Adamson was picking on another student. Jorge took it upon himself to intervene," Mr. Shadrach explains.

"So Jorge was protecting another kid from a bully. Isn't that your job?" Dad says.

"I don't deny Ian has been known to pick on weaker kids."

"Ian is a coward and a bully," I say.

Dad puts his hand on my knee to calm me down. "I know Jorge has been in a few scraps this year," he says to the principal. "But every time he is, he's protecting another kid."

"We can't have a vigilante roaming the halls. I'm afraid I'm going to have to expel Jorge from school."

"Expel?" Dad and I say at the same time.

"Jorge needs help with his anger issues," Mr. Shadrach says.

"*My anger?*" I say, getting out of my chair. "What about Ian?"

"This is exactly what I'm talking about," Mr. Shadrach says. "Jorge, you have a good heart. But you need to learn to control your temper. Mr. Gomez, I suggest you take your son to a counsellor. Help him figure out the causes of this behaviour."

"Are you calling Jorge psycho?"

"Not in the least. But he needs tools that help him control himself when he gets upset. If a teacher hadn't pulled him off Ian, Jorge could be facing an assault charge."

"That bad, huh?" Dad asks.

"That bad," Mr. Shadrach replies.

Dad whistles. "I didn't know you had it in you,"

he says to me. "Thanks, Mr. Shadrach. Tell the principal you're sorry, Jorge."

"Sorry, Mr. Shadrach."

"Don't apologize to me," the principal says. "Apologize to your parents. They're the ones you're hurting."

♥ ♥ ♥

I stand outside our van, waiting for Dad to unlock it.

"Hold on a second," he says. He pulls out his cigarettes.

"Mom will kill you if she sees you with one of those."

"Yeah, we know where you get your temper from. She's going to hit the roof when she finds out you've been expelled." Dad lights the cigarette and takes a deep breath. "What is with you, Jorge? You've been as quiet as churchmouse for seventeen years. And now you're punching everything that moves."

"That's not true."

"Yes it is. I know what your principal was talking about. Your mother has noticed it too. It's like a light switch. All at once you go to this dark place. It's scary."

It's hard to hear Dad say this. I don't have a lot of friends. Dad is like a buddy to me.

"Is it your grades?" Dad asks. "We can hire a tutor if you're worried about getting into college."

"I'm not going to college," I tell him.

"Don't be like that."

"Books and numbers aren't my thing. And what for? I'm fine working at the store with you and mom."

"Then why are you so moody? What are you trying to prove?"

I hadn't been able bring myself to say it.

"Are you ashamed of something?" Dad pushed.

"Sort of. It's not as bad as you might think. But it's not what I wanted for myself."

"Jorge, if you don't tell me what's going on, I can't help you."

I walk away from the van. Dad follows me.

"Dad, I think I'm gay."

"But you're the straightest guy I know." He looks confused. "Is this why you beat the crap out of Ian Adamson?"

"I think I would have done that if I was straight. It's not like I want to be gay. But it's like fighting bullies is the only thing I have control of anymore."

"That explains a lot, actually."

"Do you hate me?"

"Of course not. I'd be lying if I said I wasn't a little sad. It's not going to be easy for you. But I don't hate you. And your mother won't either, I promise you that. But you need to control your emotions. If you can't, you're going to be really popular in prison. Come here. Give me a hug."

The hug is awkward but heartfelt.

"You know Mom is going to smell the smoke on your clothes, right?" I say to him.

"She's not going to care when I tell her you were expelled."

02 Kid Romeo

THE PARKING LOT LIGHTS LOOK LIKE spongy white balls through the foggy windshield as I drive up. The warehouse is in an industrial park. You know, the kind you pass along the highway on your way to someplace else. Each unit is marked by a glass door next to a loading bay.

There's no sign or even a sandwich board. I squint to compare the peeling black numbers on the glass door to the Google map I printed. The numbers match. This is it: The School of Hard Knocks.

A doorbell buzzes as the glass door closes behind me, like I'm entering a corner store. I poke my head through the doorway on my right. There's a beat-up old wrestling ring beneath bright florescent lights. The ropes are wrapped with electrical tape. The padding covering the corner turnbuckles are ripped in places. A muscular bald man is leading a girl and three guys through some stretches.

"Hey, Romeo," the girl says, getting the bald man's attention. She points to me.

I wave at them like I don't understand English.

"Jorge?" the man asks me.

"That's me. Kid Romeo?" I ask, hoping my voice doesn't crack.

"Kid Romeo to my friends. Romeo Stallone to my enemies. I was starting to think you weren't coming."

"It's dark. This place is hard to find."

Romeo vaults over the top rope like a superhero. He lands firmly on the padded floor in front of me and calls over his shoulder. "Arshdeep! Finish the warmup for me while I show Jorge around."

Romeo takes me into his office. The walls are covered with wrestling posters that go as far back as the eighties.

"What kind of name is Jorge? Mexican?"

"Portuguese," I say, looking around. "Is that you?" I ask, pointing at one of the posters.

"Yeah. I wasn't much older than you are now when that picture was taken," Romeo says.

"My dad used to watch you on All Star Wrestling."

"You're making me feel old. Did your parents sign the permission slip I emailed you?"

I fish the folded paper from my backpack and hand it to Romeo. He scans the form and then puts it on a desk cluttered with posters and receipts.

"I'll call your parents tomorrow to make sure you didn't forge their names," Romeo says. "Get dressed and meet me back in the ring."

"Where do I change?" I ask.

"Right here. But leave your bag in the gym where you can keep an eye on it," Romeo says.

I pull myself up to the ring apron and step into the ring. I bounce up and down like it's the surface of the moon.

"Feels like coming home doesn't it?" Romeo says.

"It does," I say.

"Let me introduce you to the family," Romeo says. "This ugly thing here is Troll. That's his girlfriend, Brittany. The guy who looks like a totem pole is Thunder. And that dark hulk over there is Arshdeep. Everybody, this is George with a J."

The other students nod and mumble hello.

"Be nice to him. I need the money," Romeo says. "Everyone line up in the corner. We're going to run the ropes."

I fall in line behind the other wrestlers. I watch as Thunder throws himself into the ropes and lets them propel him across the ring. He does this ten times before he tags in Troll.

Running the ropes takes more coordination than it seems. You have to spin around at just the right time, and remember to grab the top rope so you don't fall out of the ring. The ropes aren't stretchy. They feel like steel cables when you bounce off them. On my last try, I hook my right foot on the bottom rope and fall flat on my face.

"Ouch," I say into the ring apron.

"Stop worrying about how you look. You'll get it in no time," Romeo says. "Now meet Thunder and me outside the ring on the mats."

Romeo holds the ropes open for me to step out of the ring. Thunder is already waiting on the wrestling mats.

"Now I'm going to take you through the basics of a wrestling match," Romeo says. "Remember, pro wrestling is like real life. The bad guy — we call him the Heel — always cheats to win. The good guy, or the Face, always plays by the rules. The Face takes control of the match to start, and then the Heel gets the upper hand by cheating. And just when the Face starts to make his comeback and looks like he's going to win the match, the Heel uses a dirty trick to steal the victory."

"Wow. That *is* just like real life," I say.

"I know, right? Now you're going to learn the collar-and-elbow lockup. If this doesn't look good, then you've lost the marks before the match has even started. A mark is someone who takes their wrestling very seriously," Romeo explains. "They come to all the shows and read all the blogs. You need to pay attention to them, just as much as you need to pay attention to what's going on in the ring."

Romeo takes me through a collar-and-elbow lockup. He places my left hand on Thunder's elbow and my right hand behind his neck. Thunder and I practise a few times. We clunk heads once. It hurts like hell.

Once Romeo is convinced I've mastered the move, he shows me how to put Thunder into a headlock and flip him onto the mat.

"Make sure your heels hit the mat flat or you're going to screw up your ankles," Romeo warns me.

Thunder and I move in and pretend to jockey for control. Thunder reeks of sweat. Without warning, he flips me over onto the mat. My heels crash into the rubber, sending lightning rods of pain up my legs.

"That's not what I told you to do!" Romeo says to Thunder. "You practically smashed Jorge's ankles into the ground!"

"I'm fine," I say.

The session ends with the other students doing a practice match. They tag each other in when they get tired. Romeo and I sit on the bleachers and watch the action in the ring.

"So what did you think?" Romeo asks.

"That was the most fun I've had in my life," I say.

"Then let me be the first to welcome you to the Canadian Pacific Wrestling Federation." Romeo smiles and slaps me on the shoulder.

03 Cloverdale

PART OF TRAINING TO BECOME a pro wrestler is helping set up and take down the shows. The Cloverdale show is the first show since I started training at the School of Hard Knocks. To make a good impression, I begged my parents to give me the day off work from the store and to let me borrow the store van.

I get up at the crack of dawn. Arshdeep and I have to transport the ring to the Cloverdale Fairgrounds. We have become fast friends since I started training.

We've been lifting weights together and training in the ring on our own time whenever we can. The extra practice has done wonders for my confidence.

"Have you thought about your gimmick for the student show yet?" Arshdeep asks.

"It's all I think about. Every idea I have has been done a million times over: a Mountie, a fireman, a businessman . . ."

"Dude, those are gimmicks for strippers."

"I want to come up with a gimmick that doesn't age. Like John Cena."

"Don't make yourself nuts about it. The whole point of a student show is to try things out."

"I'm really nervous about talking into the mic before the match," I confess.

"I hate to say it, bro. But you're really awful at trash talk."

"I can't help it. I used to stutter as a kid."

"Talking trash is like running the ropes. If you think about it too much you'll trip and fall."

"What's your gimmick?"

"I'm a hot South Asian guy. Can't you tell?"

Yeah. I could.

"I started out as a terrorist but my dad put his foot down."

"He didn't want you to support stereotypes?"

"Yeah. And we're Sikh."

"Hey, Lion's Gate Wrestling is having a show next week at The Wise Hall. Want to go?"

Lions Gate Wrestling is the other local wrestling federation. I looked into training with them, but it was too expensive.

"Sure," says Arshdeep. "But don't tell Romeo. He can't stand Ricky Flamingo."

"I got that impression. What's the deal?"

"A long time ago, in a wrestling ring far, far, away, Ricky Flamingo trained at the School of Hard Knocks. Romeo took Ricky under his wing and showed him everything he knew about the business. Then as soon as he could, Ricky started his own fed, and poached Romeo's best wrestler Kyle O'Malley."

"Romeo trained Kyle O'Malley?" Kyle O'Malley is a god in the indy circuit.

"You wouldn't know it from LGW's website. He's the poster child for their school."

"I wanted to train there for that reason."

"If you ever want Romeo to give you a hundred push-ups, tell him that."

❤ ❤ ❤

It takes Romeo, Arshdeep, Troll, Brittany and me most of the day to set up the ring. Thunder shows up just as we're putting on the finishing touches. The first thing Thunder does when he enters the auditorium is jump into the ring and start running the ropes.

"Get your lazy butt out of that ring!" Romeo shouts. "You don't pitch in, you don't get to show off."

"But I'm practically a worker," Thunder says. He thinks he's such a star. "I shouldn't have to help set up."

"You're not a worker until you make your debut," Romeo tells him. "Now get out of my ring. The rest of you relax before the show."

Arshdeep and I wander off to the concession stand. A good-looking black guy behind the counter is counting cash for the till. He looks about my age. His plaid shirt is so clean and crisp it could have come right from the store.

I watch him as he sweeps one loonie at a time from the counter into the palm of his hand. It's hypnotic. His lips move as he adds up the pile. I imagine what it would be like to kiss them.

"Is it too early to get a Coke?" Arshdeep's voice brings both the cashier and me back to reality.

"You made me lose my count," the guy says. He looks like he's about to give Arshdeep the what for. But his eyes meet mine and his face relaxes into a smile.

I look away, embarrassed. "Sorry, we didn't mean to interrupt you," I say.

"So can we get a Coke or not?" Arshdeep asks.

"Sure thing," he says. He puts the till in the cash register and goes to pour us each a Coke. "I have to change the syrup. I'll be right back."

Once he leaves, Arshdeep says to me, "That guy was totally checking you out, bro."

"What?"

"That guy wants to have sex with you. Didn't you see the way he was looking at you?"

"Your blood sugar must be low. You're imagining things, Arshdeep."

The guy comes back and pours us two cups of Coke. "On the house," he says. "I saw how hard you guys were working."

His hand touches mine when he gives me my Coke. I can feel myself blushing. This is stupid. What are the odds of meeting another gay guy in Cloverdale? Crazier still, what are the odds of a guy this good-looking being attracted to me?

"Are you two wrestling tonight?" he asks.

I'm too nervous to speak.

"We're still training," Arshdeep tells him.

"But we're doing a student show next week. You should come check it out. It's Jorge's first match."

"Sounds like fun. George is your name?" he asks me.

"With a J. Like Jesus," Arshdeep answers. He is loving this. I want to punch him, not to hurt him, but to make him stop.

"I'm Thom," the guy behind the counter says.

"Pleased to meet you. I'm Arshdeep. If you're interested in coming to our show, you can find the event on Facebook. Look for the School of Hard Knocks."

"I'll do that," Thom says.

We take our Cokes and walk toward the bleachers. Arshdeep can't stop laughing. I elbow him to get him to stop. But he only laughs harder.

"It's not funny," I tell him.

"It's perfect. You haven't stepped in the ring and you already have a fan."

I look back at Thom. He's still staring and smiling. Without even thinking, I smile back and wave.

Arshdeep stops so abruptly he nearly drops his Coke. "Hold the phone." Arshdeep looks back at Thom and then at me. "Are you . . .?"

I pull Arshdeep away so no one can hear us.

"Yes! I'm gay," I whisper. "I'm sorry I didn't tell you sooner. We've been spending so much time together. I didn't want you to get the wrong impression."

"No, this is cool. My girlfriend, Pria, is going to be so impressed when I tell her I set up a gay guy on a date."

"Don't get too excited. I've haven't kissed a girl, much less another guy."

"Dude, trust me. If that guy's eyes were a pair of lips, you would be French kissing by now."

I have to admit hearing Arshdeep say that makes me feel kind of hot. But this isn't the time or place to be thinking about guys. For all I know, Thom will have forgotten me by the time he gets home from work.

04 Student Show

I TRY TALKING MY DAD out of coming to the student show. But he won't take no for answer.

It was Dad who got me into pro wrestling. He used to watch it with *his* father after they came to Canada from Portugal. Grandpa loved watching wrestling because he didn't need to know English to understand what was going on.

The School of Hard Knocks has taken both our minds off me being gay and getting expelled from school. Sometimes I worry that my training is our way of not talking about what's going on. But my parents insist I can talk to them about anything. It's me. I don't know if I'm ready yet.

The chime on the glass door rings as Dad and I enter the school. Romeo is talking to volunteers who are helping out with the show.

"Hey, Jorge!" Romeo says. "Ready for your debut?"

"My knees won't stop shaking," I tell him. "Romeo, this is my dad, Manny Gomez."

Dad is starstruck. He can't seem to speak.

"Pleasure to meet you," Romeo says. "You have a talented son here."

"The pleasure is all mine!" Dad says, finding his voice. "I think I saw every match between you and Gene Kiniski back in the seventies."

"Gene taught me everything I know. I cried like a baby when he died."

"Those were the good old days of wrestling. No smoke machines and fireworks. Just good old-fashioned wrestling," Dad says.

"Okay, Dad, put your tongue back in your mouth," I say. "I need to get ready for the show."

"How much is the ticket?" Dad asks.

"Your money's no good here," Romeo tells him.

"Let me give you twenty dollars," Dad says, trying to force the bill into Romeo's hand.

"Dad!" I drag my finger across my neck to get him to cut it out. He gets the hint and takes a seat on the bleachers.

Romeo puts me up against the Atom Bomb for my first match. Atom and Romeo trained together in the seventies. Atom weighs about 300 pounds. His arms are as big as my thighs.

"Are you kidding me?" I say when Romeo introduces me to Atom.

"Everyone starts off against Atom," Romeo says. "He's indestructible. And he'll punish you if you don't do as you're told."

"How's it going?" Atom says. I'm surprised by his voice, which is quite gentle.

Atom and I spend the next fifteen minutes going through the match. He keeps things pretty simple. We focus on the holds and moves I've already perfected.

"I'm going to give you a piece of advice," Atom says. He opens the curtain between the hall and the gym. "See those two big ladies sitting in the front row?"

"The ones with the fanny packs around their stomachs?"

Atom nods. "Those are the Schlepp sisters. They come to every show. It doesn't matter what it is. They're true marks. If they love you or hate you, you're wrestling gold in this town."

My match with Atom is third on the roster. I run through the order of our match in my head. I go over the moves, acting them out in my brain. Then I hear the ring announcer try to pronounce my name, "And hailing from Vancouver . . ."

Oh my God! I've been so nervous about the

match, I forgot to tell the announcer my name is pronounced "George."

"Hair-gay . . . your-gay?" the announcer says. The crowd starts to laugh as he continues to butcher my name.

"GEORGE!" my father finally shouts. This is getting worse by the second.

"George!" the announcer says.

I burst through a black curtain and enter the gym. The first people I see are the Schlepp sisters. They both start shouting, "You're gay! You're gay!"

This is exactly what I was afraid of when I signed up to become a pro wrestler. I want to run back through the curtain and hide.

Then I see Thom from the Cloverdale fairgrounds sitting behind my dad.

I can't believe he actually came to see me wrestle. Either he's insane or he likes me. Now I really have to put on a good show. I bound over the top rope to impress him.

Atom storms through the curtain like he's ready

to eat everyone alive. He stops in front of the Schlepp sisters and starts yelling in their faces. Where is the soft-spoken guy I practised with? He's like Jekyll and Hyde. I'm genuinely afraid.

The bell rings, starting the match. I take control of Atom. He pretends to get frustrated that he can't get the upper hand. On cue, he rakes my eyes with his fingers and starts pounding on me.

My time to shine arrives with my "hot comeback." That's the point in every match when it seems the Face might actually win. I hit Atom with a couple of flying dropkicks. Then I do a backwards somersault from the top rope.

Atom lifts his legs and I land across his knees. He picks me up and body slams my back to the mat. Atom finishes me off with a belly flop off the second rope. He pins me: 1-2-3.

The crowd boos as Atom's hand is raised for the win. I roll out under the bottom rope, pretending I'm more beat up than I am. I dash back behind the curtain into the dressing room.

"You were awesome!" Atom says when he joins me out of sight of the audience.

"Thanks!" I say. "I barely felt you when you landed on top of me."

"I'm a pro."

I towel off and change back into my street clothes. I'm pumped up with adrenaline. And I'm relieved I got through my match without getting hurt.

After the show, all the wrestlers go out into the audience to say hi to our friends and fans.

"I didn't know you could do a backward somersault!" my dad says when he sees me.

Out of the corner of my eye, I can see Thom lurking nearby. He looks out of place amongst the likes of the Schlepp sisters.

"I've been practising for weeks," I tell Dad. "Hey, do you mind if I say hello to someone really quick?"

"Go ahead," Dad says.

I'm more nervous about talking to Thom than I was to fight my first match. I'm afraid to look at him.

"So what did you think?" I ask him.

"I'm impressed. Yours was the best match by far," he says. "Could we talk in private for a minute?"

"Sure."

We go out to the parking lot.

"I was wondering if you would like to go out sometime," Thom says.

"Out?"

"Like on a date. I could be totally misreading the whole situation. But I got a vibe from you the other day."

"A vibe?"

"This is so embarrassing. I knew I shouldn't have come here."

"No, no, no . . . it's cool," I whisper. "I'm not really out to the other wrestlers."

"I just assumed from your friend's behaviour at Cloverdale . . ."

"He had no idea until I told him later."

"That must have been awkward."

"You did me a favour."

"So is that a yes?"

"Totally."

"I can't believe this worked. I was sure you were going to punch me in the face. Let me give you my number. Call or text me whenever you feel like. No pressure."

"I'll call you tonight when I get home."

Arshdeep is standing with my father when I go back inside the school.

"Was that who I think it was?" Arshdeep asks.

"Yup." I can't keep myself from smiling.

"Who are you guys talking about?" Dad asks. "What did I miss?"

"I'll tell you all about it on the drive home," I tell him.

I'm so happy right now, I want to do another somersault off the top rope.

05 First Date

"HEY, THOM!" I SAY as I enter the store through the back. Our shop, the Union Market, is basically a big old house. The store is on the ground floor. My parents and I live in the two floors above.

"Thom was telling me how you guys met," Dad says.

"Your father went a whole five minutes without making a fool of himself," Mom says.

"A new record," I say.

"See what I put up with?" Dad says to Thom.

"I love your store! We don't have anything like this in Surrey," says Thom.

"You and Jorge should open one after you get married," Mom says, winking at me.

"And that's our cue to leave," I say. I take Thom by the arm.

"Nice meeting you, Mr. and Mrs. Gomez!"

"Don't encourage them," I say.

We walk down the sidewalk toward Thom's car. He clicks a small black remote that triggers an electronic chirp.

"This is us," Thom says.

"You drive a Mercedes?"

"It's used."

"I drive a minivan."

"I'll remember that the next time I need to go to Costco."

We drive downtown and have lunch at the Cactus Club at English Bay. It's a beautiful day out. The sun's reflection off the ocean nearly blinds me.

"So why is a guy who drives a Mercedes working at the Cloverdale fairgrounds?" I ask him.

"The pension is good."

"Very funny."

"To be honest, I decided to apply for every job on the City of Surrey website. The concession stand was the only one I was qualified for."

"Why the City? There are tons of restaurant jobs around."

"This is just a stepping stone. I want to become an environmental lawyer someday. I think it's disgusting how we treat this planet."

"So you're a crusader."

"Does that bother you?"

"Not at all. I think it's cool. Believe me, I have a history of sticking up for the underdog."

The waitress arrives with our food. I sneak looks at Thom as he spreads his napkin on his lap and tosses his pasta to let it cool.

"So why pro wrestling?" Thom asks, out of the blue. "I thought everyone was into UFC these days."

"I hate UFC. It's just two people pounding the crap out of each other until one of them passes out."

"And pro wrestling isn't?"

"Of course not. Pro wrestling is a dance. It has its own language. It takes themes from current events and acts them out in the ring. A good guy in a wrestling match is no different from you trying to protect the environment. You're going up against an opponent who will use every dirty trick in the world to get the upper hand. And all you can do is play by the rules until you win."

Thom tilts his head to his side. "I never thought of it that way. I have a new respect for wrestling now."

Thom digs into his pasta. I feel like I've passed a test.

We decide to go for a walk on the Seawall after lunch. I give my leftovers to a homeless guy digging through one of the trash cans on the beach.

"That was sweet of you," Thom says.

"We donate a lot of expired food to the soup kitchens around town," I tell him. "My parents are the good kind of Catholic."

"They seemed nice when I talked to them at the store."

"They're still getting used to this whole gay thing," I say. "You're the first person I've ever been on a date with — guy or girl."

"Really?"

"How many guys have you dated?"

"Three. I just came off a two-year relationship."

"Two years! How old are you?"

"Seventeen. How old are you?"

"Seventeen. Wow. You have way more experience at this than I do."

"Don't let it get to you. There are plenty of guys our age who haven't been in a relationship."

"So why did you guys break up?"

"It was complicated. Lionel is a great guy, and the sex was amazing . . ."

"You guys were having sex?"

"We were totally safe. If that's what you're worried about . . ."

"I've never even kissed a guy. I feel like I'm driving a car without a licence."

"I go to a private school. It's pretty liberal. What about you? Where do you go to school?"

"I don't."

"You graduated?"

I was hoping this wouldn't come up until we got to know each other better. But there's no point in lying. "I was expelled."

"Why?"

"Fighting. My grades weren't that great either."

Thom grows quiet.

"Does that bother you?" I ask.

"You just don't strike me as someone who gets into fights."

"I'm training to be a pro wrestler."

"But that's not real."

"Want to see the bruises?"

"You know what I mean. It takes a lot of anger to hit someone. Were you being bullied?"

"Sort of the opposite."

"You were picking on gay guys?"

"God, no. I was sort of acting like their bodyguard."

"That's noble of you."

"Tell that to the police."

"You were arrested?"

"It never got that serious. But it was headed that way. I have a hard time watching people be mean. Instead of using my words, I tend to insert myself in the situation."

"Did you hurt anyone?"

"Only in self-defence. I know how awful this must sound. I'm totally ashamed of myself. I've been working with a counsellor. It's one of the reasons I started pro wrestling. My counsellor thinks I was trying to suppress my sexuality with my fists."

I feel like I've blown the date. I shouldn't have agreed to this. Who am I kidding? Thom is way out of my league.

He doesn't say anything for a few minutes. So I ask, "Why *did* you break up with your boyfriend?"

"Because the only reason we were dating was that we looked good together."

"Do you still see him?"

"At school mostly. He took the breakup pretty hard. He's convinced we'll get back together. But it's over as far as I'm concerned."

"So I'm your rebound date."

"Maybe. I don't know. You seemed really sweet when I met you at the fairgrounds. And you're so far removed from my world. I was intrigued. I thought we might click."

Why do I get the feeling he doesn't think we click? Maybe because deep down, I know that we don't.

I do want to get to know him better. It takes a lot of courage to dedicate your life to something as impossible as protecting the planet. I need to be around someone like that.

"We should get going," Thom says. "I have a long drive back to Surrey."

"Sure thing."

We walk back to the car without speaking. I don't know what to say to make him like me again. I feel like a freak. I just want this to be over now.

Thom drops me off in front of the store and unlocks the car door. "I'll call you," he says.

"Cool." I look at him. I don't know if I should give him a kiss or a hug, so I just get out of the car. Something tells me I'll never see him again.

06 Sticks and Stones

"JORGE! YOU LOOK LIKE you're moving through water!" Romeo screams at me. I am botching another drill during practice.

"What's with you today?" Arshdeep asks when I get to the corner. "You look like someone kicked you in the balls."

"It's been a week since I went on my date with you-know-who. And he still hasn't called or texted," I whisper.

"So call him. Maybe he's playing hard to get," Arshdeep says. "My girlfriend, Pria, made me jump through hoops before she went on a second date with me."

"Thom doesn't seem like he's into head games."

"Then screw him. There's plenty more where that came from," Arshdeep says.

Thunder finishes the drill and gets behind us in line in the corner. "What are you two girls gossiping about?"

"How sloppy you are in the ring," Arshdeep says. He steps through the ropes for his turn to do the drill.

"That guy is so full of himself," Thunder says.

"He has the moves to back it up," I reply.

My mind switches from Thunder back to Thom. Maybe Arshdeep is right. There are lots of fish in the sea. I can't just hand my heart over to the first guy I meet. For all I know Thom is back together with his boyfriend. They are probably laughing about the date Thom went on with the high-school dropout training to be a pro wrestler.

But inside, I know Thom wouldn't be so shallow as to make fun of me like that. In the few hours we were together I could the feel the connection between us. And then I had to tell him about my fighting in school. He probably thinks I'm a psycho.

I should call Thom to find out how he feels. For all I know, he's wondering why I haven't reached out to him. I've almost called him a half dozen times. Then I chicken out before I press "call" on my phone. I've written all sorts of texts. Then I delete them before hitting "send."

I thought coming out was supposed to make my life better. But I feel like I've been kicked in the gut. I wish I had never agreed to go on a date with him.

"Okay, everyone, take ten," Romeo shouts.

We all climb out of the ring and guzzle water from our bottles. I towel off and check my phone for messages. There's a missed call! Oh my God! Thom called me!

"I'll be right back," I tell Romeo. "I have to make an important call." "We start in five minutes," he warns.

I go outside. My sweaty body freezes in the chilly March air. I dial Thom's number.

"Hi," Thom says, all peaches and cream. "I'm glad you called me back. I was worried you were avoiding me."

"I'm at wrestling practice."

"So that's why you sound out of breath. I thought you were happy to hear from me."

"I am. I was working up the nerve to call you to see if you wanted to go out again."

"Actually, I was calling to see if you would be interested in going to a protest with me on Sunday."

"What kind of protest?"

"The pipeline."

Pipeline? Which pipeline? There are so many.

"Sure," I tell him.

Romeo sticks his head out the door. "Are you coming back in to practice? Or are you going to gossip on the phone all night?"

I hold up my finger.

"I have to get back in the ring," I tell Thom. "Can you text me the details?"

"Sure thing," Thom says.

"I'm glad you called."

"I'm glad you called back."

"Talk soon."

I jump for joy and shout, "Yahoo!" at the stars. Then the cold attacks the sweat on my skin and I run back inside.

Arshdeep grabs me by the shoulders as soon as I enter the gym. "You missed the big announcement! Romeo said I'm going to make my pro debut at next month's show!"

"That's awesome, Arshdeep! We should go celebrate after practice."

"For sure!"

I can see that Thunder is fuming. I'm sure he was expecting Romeo to put him in the next show.

The second half of practice is amazing. There's a spring in my step. All my moves pop like fireworks. I can't remember when I felt this good about myself.

Thunder is still pissed that he's been passed over for a spot in the next show. The angrier Thunder gets, the stiffer his punches and uppercuts get. Every time I'm paired up against him, I have to be careful. I don't want him to give me a black eye before my next date with Thom.

The session ends with practice matches. Thankfully Romeo puts me up against Troll. Our match goes pretty well, but I wouldn't charge anyone to watch it.

The next practice match is between Thunder and Arshdeep. You can feel the anger rolling off Thunder like a storm. His hands are balled into fists. He's asking for trouble. I know Arshdeep can handle himself in the ring, but I have a bad feeling about this.

The match seems to be going fine. Thunder still has steam coming out of his nostrils but Arshdeep is like a dancer in the ring. He can make anything look good.

Halfway through the match Thunder lifts Arshdeep for a body slam. Arshdeep's head is pointed toward the floor and his stomach is against Thunder's chest. Then Thunder bends Arshdeep's arm behind his back. All of us watching gasp, including Romeo. This is a risky move even for a veteran. It's not the type of thing you do on a whim.

"Wait! Wait! Wait!" Arshdeep shouts. Thunder ignores Arshdeep's protests and drops him into the mat.

CRACK!

I grab my arm in sympathy pain. Thunder stands over Arshdeep who is writhing in pain. Romeo hops over the top rope into the ring. He pushes Thunder out of the way and kneels down next to Arshdeep.

"Grab the first aid kit and the ice packs from the freezer!" Romeo shouts.

I run to the office and grab a couple of ice packs from the old fridge. Romeo puts the packs on Arshdeep's shoulder. He tells me to start his car so we can take him to the hospital.

I see Thunder standing in the corner on my way out of the ring. I swear there's hint of a smile on his face.

07 The Protest

THERE ARE ABOUT 500 PEOPLE in front of the Vancouver Art Gallery. They are voicing their anger about the proposed pipeline. I've never been to a protest before so I'm not sure what I'm supposed to do.

"What do you mean you've never been to a protest before?" Thom says when I tell him that.

"I'm a shy guy. I don't like crowds. I get nervous speaking into the microphone at the drive thru."

"How is it you can wrestle in front of a mob

of angry wrestling fans but you don't like crowds?" Thom says.

"When I wrestle there are ropes between me and the audience."

"Just repeat what the crowd says, and cheer after someone speaks."

"That sounds more like a dictatorship than a protest," I observe.

"Don't get smart with me or I'll have to put you in a headlock."

"You don't have to get aggressive to touch me."

"I'll remember that," Thom purrs into my ear. "How's Arshdeep?"

"He's pretty depressed that he can't wrestle for six weeks. I want to drive out to Burnaby to cheer him up."

"It sucks that he's not going to be able to be in the show."

"It's a wrestling card, not a show."

"Tomayto, tomahto. It still sucks."

"At least Romeo kicked Thunder out of the School of Hard Knocks. Rumour has it he marched right over to Lion's Gate Wrestling. He's working as a manager there."

"That sounds like a promotion to me."

"He's basically an extra."

We listen to a few more speeches and rhyme off a few more chants with the crowd. Then I ask Thom, "Have you told your parents about me yet?"

"They know I met someone."

"But you haven't told them that I'm a high-school dropout. Or that I'm training to become a pro wrestler."

"It hasn't come up yet."

"Do they know my name?"

"They know you have one."

I don't know how to respond to that. Maybe the protest has empowered me, so I just say what's on my mind. "Do I embarrass you?"

"Why do you think that?"

"Look at us. You're wearing a hundred-dollar shirt. I got mine on sale at Old Navy."

"This was a present from Lionel."

"If that's supposed to make me feel better, it's not working."

"This might shock you but my parents are quite conservative. I didn't tell them about Lionel until we had been dating for three months."

"That does shock me. You seem so confident about being gay."

"I am. But I live in Surrey. It feels like we're five years behind the rest of the world."

"Some of my relatives are still stuck in the seventies."

"But Portugal is one of the most liberal countries in the world! They legalized gay marriage and decriminalized drugs."

"Since when do you know so much about Portugal?"

"Since I started dating you."

"So we're dating?"

"Maybe," Thom says, grinning.

He kisses me on the lips. He pushes his tongue in my mouth. I freeze for a second and then I start to relax. We wrap our arms around each other and go for it.

"Fags," someone mutters as they walk past.

I feel my shoulders start to tense up.

"It's not mean if it's true, asshole!" Thom shouts in the guy's general direction.

"Thom?"

Thom turns around to see who called his name. A good-looking Asian guy weaves his way through the crowd toward us. He's dragging another guy behind him by the hand.

"Lionel?" says Thom. "You didn't tell me you were coming to the protest."

"I'm here on a date," Lionel says. "Thom, this Eddy. Eddy, this is my ex, Thom."

Eddy steps out from behind Lionel and nods hello. He is as good-looking as Lionel.

"What a coincidence," Thom says. "I'm here on a date too! This is Jorge."

"Great turnout, huh?" Lionel says.

"I don't know if it will do any good," Thom says. "The premier and the prime minister seem intent on pushing this thing through."

"Don't be such a cynic," Lionel says, and then turns to me. "What did you think, Jorge?"

"Of the protest? It was fun. I'm with Thom, though. I feel like this pipeline is a done deal."

"You two are made for each other," Lionel says.

"My parents own a small business. They're always getting shafted by City Hall and the Province," I explain.

Thom squeezes my hand in approval.

"Eddy and I were about to get some coffee," Lionel says. "Want to come?"

"Wouldn't you two rather be alone?" Thom asks.

Eddy's face says that he would.

"You don't mind do you, Eddy?" Lionel says, ignoring the look of agony on Eddy's face.

"That should be fine," Eddy says. But his voice is saying something else.

"Do you mind?" Thom asks me.

There's a pained look on Thom's face. He obviously doesn't know how to say "no" to Lionel. I begin to wonder if Lionel will always get the last word in our relationship.

"Lead the way," I tell Lionel.

♥ ♥ ♥

At the coffee shop, Thom asks, "So how did you two meet?"

"Dating app," Lionel says.

"I thought you hated those things," Thom says.

"It's not like there are a ton of queer spaces for teens. Unless you want to sneak into a gay bar. How about you two?"

"A wrestling show at the fairgrounds," Thom says.

"You hate pro wrestling!" Lionel says. "You told me it's for morons."

"Actually Jorge is a pro wrestler," Thom says. Is he trying to one-up Lionel?

"*Training* to be a pro wrestler," I correct him.

"Tell Lionel what you told me about good guys and bad guys," Thom says. He nudges me like it's the greatest story in the world.

Thom seems like he's trying to make up for

something. I don't like it.

"Yeah, Jorge. Explain pro wrestling to me," Lionel says. He has a cocky grin on his face.

Well, if Lionel is going to be a smartass about this . . .

"At its heart, pro wrestling is a tale of good versus evil. The little guy is constantly being tested by the big guy until the little guy finally wins," I explain. "It's like the protest we were just at. The oil companies are the bad guys. We call them the Heel in pro wrestling. The protestors are the good guys, or the Face. And like real life, the fight is never really over."

"And what's your role in this battle?" Lionel asks.

"I don't know yet. But I want to be the good guy. Most wrestlers want to be a Heel because they get more money and fame."

"Just like real life," Thom says.

"Why would you want to be the good guy if all it gets you is walked over?" Lionel says.

"We don't always get to choose the roles we play," I tell him. "Besides, being gay, we're always treated as the bad guys. Like we're asking too much by expecting to be treated like human beings. Is it really too much to ask to be gay and the hero?"

"I just think it's silly to parade yourself in front of an audience pretending you're something you're not," Lionel says.

"Would you say that to a drag queen?" I ask.

There's a silence. I expect Lionel to make some bitchy comment. But he doesn't.

Back in the car Thom leans over. He gives me a peck on the cheek.

"That was beautiful the way you shot Lionel down," he says.

"Thanks," I say. "But I have to ask. You're not into me to fulfill a boyhood fantasy, are you?"

"What do you mean?"

"The way you bragged that I was a wrestler to Lionel. It sort of made me feel like one of those stuffed animals you win at the Pacific National Exhibition."

"I got a little flustered. Lionel can be a real jerk sometimes."

"Tell me about it."

"I'd be lying if I denied that part of what attracted me is that you and Lionel are night and day. But that's not what this is about. From the moment I saw you I felt something true and honest. I knew if I didn't go for it, I would spend the rest of my life kicking myself."

"When you put it that way . . . I guess that's all right."

We start to make out in the front seat of the car. Thom puts his hands down my pants but I stop him.

"Sorry," I tell him. "I'm not ready for that yet."

"I understand. Is it okay if we kiss some more?"

"Definitely."

I open my coat so I can feel Thom's arms around me. I can't believe I got the two things I want most at the same time: a boyfriend and a shot at becoming a wrestler.

08 *The Push*

ROMEO HAS ME UP AGAINST Golden Adonis in the next student show. Adonis has been with Canadian Pacific Wrestling Federation for a couple of years. He's one of the few wrestlers in Romeo's fed who is under forty. Romeo wants me to try my hand at being a Heel. Adonis is the most popular Face on his roster.

"Just because you're the Heel doesn't mean you get to call the match," Romeo tells me. "Adonis is a worker, so whatever he says goes."

"Got it."

"Adonis, I need you to work with Jorge and help him shoot on the stick to get some heat going before the match starts," Romeo says. Shoot on the stick is wrestle-talk for using the microphone to talk trash about your opponent.

"But I hate talking on the mic," I say.

"You're going to have learn sooner or later, Jorge," Romeo says. "You need to start working on your gimmick now that Arshdeep is out of commission."

"Are you saying what I think you're saying?" I ask.

"That's right, I'm giving you Arshdeep's spot in the next card."

"Awesome!" Adonis says, shaking my hand. "Good work."

"This is only a trial run," Romeo says. "You screw this up and it's back to the bush leagues."

I'm speechless. I wasn't expecting to make my debut for another three months at least. I want to call Dad and tell him. But he's sitting in the bleachers with Thom and Arshdeep.

Arshdeep . . . I wonder if Romeo has told him yet. Suddenly I feel awful. This was not how I wanted to make my pro debut, taking Arshdeep's chance.

"Let's go through the match," Adonis says, snapping me out of my head.

Adonis and I spend the next ten minutes working out what we're going to do in the ring. We're both high-flyers so there's the potential for a lot of excitement.

"What are you going to say on the stick?" Adonis asks me while we wait for our match to start.

"No idea."

"Don't overthink it," Adonis says. "Just say the first thing that comes into your head."

I listen to the audience as Atom Bomb tears Troll a new hole in the ring. When he dives onto Troll from the second rope and covers him for the pin, it sounds like he's going to go through the apron.

"All yours, boys," Atom says as he comes back through the black curtain.

The announcer stands in front of the ring. He introduces me with the name I chose. "Hailing from Whitehorse, Yukon . . . Chinook!"

I run through the curtain. The announcer covers the mic with his hand and whispers, "You need a new ring name. That one sucks."

My cheeks go red. I grab the mic from the announcer and drop it immediately. Everyone plugs their ears because of the feedback. I can see Dad hiding his eyes in embarrassment. Arshdeep and Thom are trying not to laugh.

"You suck!" one of the Schlepp sisters shouts at me. This is not how I wanted to get heat.

I pick up the mic and fumble with it some more. Then I get it in front of my mouth. My hands are shaking like a leaf.

"I-I just want you all to know that by the time I'm done with A-Adonis, he's going to need more b-b-Botox than the Real Housewives of Vancouver."

"You talk like a baby!" the other Schlepp sister shouts.

"That was personal," I say. I break my gimmick and speak in my regular voice.

The announcer grabs the mic from me before I can shame myself more. "And now for the main attraction . . . Golden Adonis!"

Adonis bursts through the curtain. The regular fans get up on their feet to cheer him into the ring. I feel small standing in my corner, waiting for him to finish making his entrance.

The bell rings. We circle each other and lock up.

"Don't sweat your entrance," Adonis whispers in my ear. "Just focus on the match."

It takes me a few minutes to shake off my embarrassment. Adonis is a master in the ring, but I manage to hold my own. The high point of the match is when I throw Adonis out of the ring, then leap over the top rope and land across his chest as he gets up from the floor. One of the Schlepp sisters applauds. I'm finally connecting with the crowd. Adonis wins the match, but I've made my mark.

Thom winks at me as I walk past him to go backstage. I wink back at him. I can't believe my boyfriend is in the audience and the marks don't even know it.

Atom Bomb pulls me aside after the show. He looks around to make sure no one else can hear and says, "Was that your boyfriend you winked at?"

Crap. I didn't think anyone saw that.

"I'm not judging," Atom says. "But I'm talking as one gay guy to another. If you want to make it in this business, don't let the marks know. It will kill your career. I've seen it happen a million times."

"You're gay! Does Romeo know?"

"My husband and I had dinner with Romeo and his wife last night."

Atom walks out of the dressing room without another word. I follow Atom into the gym. I'm stopped by a short guy in his late teens wearing a C.M. Punk shirt.

"Great match!" he says. "How long have you been training?"

"Almost four months. I'm making my debut next month."

"You're a natural in the ring. I'll keep an eye out for you," he says, and he leaves the gym.

"What did Bobby Bentley say to you?" Arshdeep asks.

"Who's Bobby Bentley?"

"The guy in the C.M. Punk shirt."

"He liked my match."

"Dude! Bobby Bentley is the top wrestling blogger in the Pacific Northwest! You get his seal of approval and you're on your way."

"Now I don't feel so bad about my lousy entrance," I say.

"You don't get off that easy. That was awful," Dad says.

"Did Jorge tell you his good news?" Romeo says, joining our conversation. "I'm putting him in the next show!"

Dad and Thom's faces light up.

Arshdeep looks confused. "But he's been in only two student shows," he says.

"Jorge has got the moves down. And he's getting heat from the crowd," says Romeo. "You saw Shirley Schlepp today. She peed her sweatpants during that match. Trust me. I had to Windex her chair."

Arshdeep still looks stunned.

"Don't worry," Romeo tells him. "You'll make your debut as soon as your doctor gives you the thumbs up."

"Sorry, Jorge. I wasn't trying to be a jerk," Arshdeep says.

"It's okay. I feel bad about taking your spot."

"No one is taking anyone's spot," Romeo says. "It's the way things are. Trust me, once Arshdeep is one hundred per cent, I'm planning a huge feud between the two of you."

Thom walks Dad and me back to the minivan.

Thom leans in to give me a peck on the cheek but I back away.

"Something wrong?" he asks.

"We better not do that here. I'll call you to explain."

Thom looks hurt and confused.

Will it always have to be like this? I start to worry that one day I'm going to have to choose between what I love doing and the guy I love being with.

09 Meet the Parents

THOM AND I MAKE A DEAL when I tell him the marks can't find out I'm gay. He will avoid displays of affection at wrestling events. I will come have dinner with his parents.

Thom lives in Rosemary Heights, the richest part of Surrey. My neighbourhood, Strathcona, has been okay for about ten years. Before that it was mostly addicts and sex trade workers.

The street looks deserted when I pull up in front

of his house. There are no cars parked along the curb. There are hardly any signs that people actually live here. Every other lawn has a For Sale sign on it. It's kind of eerie.

Thom's mom answers the door. She is a tall, beautiful black woman. Her smile reminds me of Mrs. Johnson, the Grade Two teacher who helped me with my stutter.

"You must be Jorge," she says.

"I'm here to find out if you've found Jesus."

Thom's mom looks horrified.

"Just kidding," I say.

"I'm Irma. Thomas didn't tell us you were a comedian." She does not sound amused.

"These are for you." I hand her the flowers I brought from the shop.

"How lovely," she says. "Come in."

The house is amazing. I try not to gawk. The art on the wall is original and the furniture looks handmade. The air is filled with the scent of herbs and spices. I have the urge to put on slippers and smoke a pipe.

A large, muscular black man comes down the stairs. I step back, afraid he's going to bowl me over.

"I'm John. You must be Jorge," he says.

We shake hands. It feels like my arm is going to come out of the socket.

"Thanks for having me," I say.

Thom is not far behind his father. He gives me a peck on the cheek and puts his arm through mine. "I'm glad you made it, Jorge."

"My mom sent these over," I say, handing him a white pastry box. "They're Portuguese custard tarts."

"Dinner will be ready in a few minutes," Irma says, taking the box. "Why don't you three get comfortable in the living room."

Thom and I sit next to each other on a leather loveseat. John sits across from us on the couch.

"Thom tells us you're training to be a pro wrestler," John says.

"Yeah. I make my debut in a couple of weeks."

"Interesting hobby," he remarks.

"It's more than a hobby. I'm hoping to make a career out of it."

"Seriously?"

"Dad!" Thom cuts in.

"You must admit," John says, "it doesn't sound like a promising career choice. I thought UFC was all the rage now."

"I get that a lot," I say.

"Pro wrestling and UFC are two different things, Dad," Thom says. "One is a form of storytelling. The other is two people beating each other to a pulp."

"Don't be ridiculous, Thomas. Pro wrestling reinforces white men's stereotypes," John says.

This is going to hell in a handbasket.

Irma comes into the living room. "What did I miss?" She takes a seat next to John.

"Thomas is trying to convince me that pro wrestling is art," John says.

"Now that's funny," Irma says. "It sounds dangerous. What will you do if you get injured and can't wrestle anymore, Jorge?"

"My parents own a store in the city. I'll work there until they die and live off the inheritance."

Thom, Irma and John's faces all drop.

"That was a joke," I say. "I love my parents. I honestly don't think like that . . ."

"Well, I hope you're better at wrestling than telling jokes," Irma says. "Shall we eat?"

I'm afraid to speak during the meal. Thom's parents are keen to find out what kind of books and movies I like. Nothing I say impresses them.

Halfway through the meal, Irma says, "I saw Lionel today at Starbucks."

"What did he have to say?" Thom asks.

"He wanted to know how your dad and I are doing. Jorge, did you know that Lionel volunteers at the David Suzuki Foundation?"

"No, I didn't," I say.

"Now there's a boy with a future," John says.

"Thom, I wish you would bring him around again," Irma says. "He's so smart and interesting."

I feel stupid sitting there taking this abuse. At dessert, they don't even bring out the custard tarts my mom made for them. It's like they can't wait to get rid of me.

I'm glad when dinner is over and I can finally go home. Thom's parents tell me it was a pleasure to meet me. I don't believe them for a second. Thom follows me to the van.

"Can we go for a drive?" he asks.

I unlock the door without saying a word. I don't know where to go or what Thom expects me to say. I haven't felt this low since I was expelled.

"I'm sorry I didn't warn you. My parents are snobs," Thom says. "But you wouldn't have come over if I had told you."

"Can you blame me?"

"Jorge, if you're going to be a part of my life you have to know who my parents are. You don't have to like each other. Just like I don't have to like that we can't show affection around your wrestling buddies."

I grip the steering wheel, trying to keep my emotions in check. He has a point, as much as I hate to admit it.

"Are you dating me to piss off your parents?" I ask him.

"What makes you think that?"

"You and I have nothing in common. I am blue collar, Thom. And I will be, for the rest of my life."

"You don't know how the rest of your life is going to turn out," Thom says. "I need to be with someone who puts his neck on the line for what he wants. And that's you."

I pull the van over to the curb. I take his hand in both of mine and kiss it.

"Sorry I doubted you," I tell him. "I'm not good at relationships."

"Who is?"

I kiss Thom on the lips. The kiss becomes more passionate. I try to embrace him. But the van's shift control is in the way.

"I want you so badly," Thom says.

"You have me."

"No. I mean I want you."

"Oh."

"Don't you want me too?"

"I do. But I don't want my first time to be in the back of my parents' van."

"Are your parents home?"

"They're always home."

"Mine too. This is really frustrating," Thom says. "Are you sure about the back of the van?"

"I would never be able to look at my parents with a straight face again," I say.

Thom starts laughing. It takes me a second but I get the joke. "Straight face."

Thom kisses me again. Every cell in my body lights up.

"Screw it," I say, putting the van into drive. I drive us back to my house as fast as I can without breaking the law.

Mom and Dad are on the couch watching TV when we come up the stairs behind the store.

"Hey there," I say, to their backs. "Is it okay if Thom spends the night?"

My dad snores. Mom doesn't move. They're both asleep.

Thom and I go back to my room. We undress to our underwear and crawl between the covers. Try as I might, I can't stop shaking. Thom is gentle and patient. When we are done, I start to cry.

"Are you okay?" Thom whispers.

"Yes. I've just never felt this close to another person before. I'm afraid of screwing this up."

"If it makes you feel any better," he says, "so am I."

10 Roar

THOM AND I ARE WALKING around Metrotown Centre shopping mall with Arshdeep and his girlfriend, Pria. Thom and Pria are hitting it off like a house on fire.

"It's refreshing to hang out with someone who knows what I go through," Pria says to Thom. We are waiting in line at Dairy Queen. "All I ever hear is wrestling this and wrestling that."

"I'll remember that the next time you want me to buy you an over-priced blouse at J. Crew,"

Arshdeep says.

"That blouse was on sale!" says Pria. "And it was a birthday present."

"An *early* birthday present. Six months early!" Arshdeep says. This is the happiest I've seen him since Thunder broke his arm.

"Your boyfriend buys you things?" Thom says.

"Damn right!" Pria says.

"I need a richer boyfriend."

"I'll pay for the ice cream. Happy?" I say to them.

"Someone is touchy," Thom says.

"We've been all over the mall looking for ideas for my gimmick," I tell them. "And we're no closer than when we started. The show is in a week!"

"You need to relax, bro. They're having you on," Arshdeep says. "Chill out with a dipped ice cream cone."

"I can't. I'm trying to cut calories before the show."

"You're worse than a girl," Pria says.

It feels good to be with the three of them.

The School of Hard Knocks is the first family I've ever had outside of my own home. Watching Arshdeep, Pria and Thom together warms my heart to the point I almost want to cry. I still can't believe how lucky I am.

The four of us are seated at a plastic table in the food court. Pria and Thom are comparing notes on how to give a blow job. They are using their ice cream cones to demonstrate. Arshdeep is enthralled with Thom's ability to put his entire cone in his mouth.

"That's incredible," Arshdeep says.

"One of the advantages of being attracted to the same sex is knowing all the soft spots," Thom says.

"Don't get any ideas, Arshdeep," Pria says.

"Guys, come on. There's kids around," I say.

"Fine, we'll stop having fun and focus all our attention on you," Pria says.

"Thank you," I say.

"You really are overthinking this," Arshdeep says. "Don't try to come up with a specific idea. Think of something broad to start and then work your way down."

"Arshdeep has a point," Thom says. "You're trying to come up with a stereotype that everyone will recognize on sight, right?"

"Exactly," Arshdeep says.

"How about a real estate agent?" Thom suggests.

"I don't like wearing ties," I tell him.

"How about a right-wing politician?" Pria suggests.

"Too much talking," I say. "I want to keep that to a minimum."

"A blogger?" Arshdeep says.

"Okay, that's the worst one so far. And you call yourself a wrestler," I say.

"How about a hipster!" Thom says.

I think about it. "I like it," I say.

"It's perfect," Arshdeep says. "It works as both a Face and a Heel."

"You could enter the ring taking selfies and texting," Pria says. "And wear a plaid shirt and grow a crazy moustache."

"Too bad you don't have time to grow a man bun," Arshdeep says.

"I draw the line at a man bun," Thom says.

"What do I wear in the ring?" I ask.

"Speedos," Thom says.

"No way! I can't stand in front of a crowd in nothing but a Speedo and kick pads!"

"But you have an amazing body," Thom says. "Take off your shirt and show Pria your torso."

"Ooh, a floor show! I should have brought some bills for a tip," Pria says.

"Take it off! Take it off! Take it off!" Thom chants. Soon Pria is chanting along with him.

"You're embarrassing me," I say.

"I'm with Jorge on this one," Arshdeep says. "It's hard enough being judged on your wrestling. But to have the marks judge your body? It's tough."

"Poor babies. Try being a woman, like anywhere on earth," Pria says.

"Jorge, do you want to make an impact? Or do you want to blend in?" Thom says.

Sticking out is what I'm worried about. Thom has a point though. I wouldn't be the first wrestler to wear just a pair of trunks in the ring. But most of those guys are on steroids.

"Now I'm really regretting eating this ice cream cone," I say.

"We've done it! High five!" Pria says. She raises her palm for Thom to slap.

"I think it's time for Jorge to model some Speedos for us," Thom says.

"This day just keeps getting better and better," Pria says.

We drive out to Burnaby Mountain Park after the mall. The weather is getting warmer. With luck we'll have an early summer.

Pria leads us higher and higher up the mountain.

"Hurry up, you pussies. I don't have all day," she says from ten feet ahead of us.

I'm nearly out of breath when we get to the top. But the view is worth it. Thom puts his arm around my shoulder. Arshdeep puts his good arm around Pria. We all take in the view.

"Okay, buddy," Arshdeep says, breaking the silence. "It's time you learn how to roar."

"Roar?" I say.

"You're too timid on the microphone. You need to get used to the sound of your own voice."

"Do we have to do this?"

"I think you know the answer to that question already."

"Thank God," Thom says. "What you did at the last student show was an absolute gong show."

"I could really use your support right now," I tell Thom.

Pria finds a dry spot of grass to take it all in and Thom joins her.

"Okay, now I just want you to roar like a lion," Arshdeep instructs me.

I do as I'm told but it's pretty lame.

"Louder. Like you mean it!"

I roar a little louder, but I feel stupid. What if

someone sees us? What will they think?

Then Arshdeep grabs me by the balls and squeezes hard. "I said *roar*. Do it so this entire valley can hear you," he says.

I let out the biggest sound I've ever made in my life. I take a deep breath and do it again.

"Say, 'I'm going to tear you from limb to limb, you stupid piece of meat!'"

"I'm going to tear you from limb to limb, you stupid piece of meat!" I repeat at the top of my lungs.

"Now, 'This is my house and you have no business being here!'"

"This is my house and you have no business being here!" I follow suit.

"Now say the first thing that comes to your mind!"

"They won't be able to use you for artisanal toast when I'm done with you!"

"You did it!" Arshdeep says.

"I did it!" I agree.

"I'm kind of turned on," Thom says.

"Me too," Pria chimes in.

I whip off my jacket and shirt. I roar at the top of my lungs. It feels good.

A hiker coming up the trail says to me, "Keep it down over there!"

"No! *You* keep it down," I shout back.

"Now I'm really turned on," Thom says.

Pria gets up from the grass and joins me in my roar. Soon all four of us are roaring into the valley. We roar until we fall onto the ground, exhausted and laughing.

11 Debut

THE SHOW DOESN'T START for another hour. I try to calm my nerves by running on the spot and doing some push-ups. There are twelve of us backstage. I'm the only newcomer of the group.

Romeo is putting me up against Adonis again to help me feel at ease. I'm relieved. Some of the other wrestlers in the fed can be real prima donnas. You would think they were wrestling at Madison Square Gardens instead of Cloverdale Fairgrounds.

"If you're not in your gimmick, get into it fast," Romeo says, coming backstage. "We're letting the marks in."

"Have you been smoking?" I ask Romeo. I can smell the cigarette fumes as he walks by.

"Yeah. That stupid Ricky Flamingo is here. Would you believe that creep offered to buy my fed? I taught that jackass everything he knows, and now he thinks he's Vince McMahon."

"Don't let him get to you," Atom Bomb says.

"I wish we sold more tickets tonight," Romeo says. "Screw him. Everybody, put on a good show. That's all that matters, right?"

I find a corner and put on my Speedo, wrestling shoes and kick pads. I've tried out my look at the School of Hard Knocks. It felt pretty cool, wrestling in next to nothing. But standing here backstage with the other wrestlers is a different matter.

"Is that your gimmick?" Atom Bomb asks me.

"Too much? Or not enough?"

"I like it!" he says.

Does he like it because I look fierce? Or because he's gay? I have to stop second-guessing myself.

"You look like a real wrestler, not one of those wannabes," Adonis assures me.

That's a relief. Still, I'm so nervous I have goosebumps and shrink dink.

"Jorge! You have a visitor," Romeo shouts.

Romeo parts the curtains slightly and lets Thom in. I'm relieved to see a friendly face. I want to hug and kiss him. But I can't with the marks just on the other side of the curtain.

"How do you feel?" Thom asks.

"Like I'm going to throw up."

"You're going to do just fine," he says. "Remember to roar. Is there anything I can do for you?"

"Can you help me with my wrist tape? I keep making a mess of it."

Thom spends the next few minutes wrapping fabric tape around my wrists. I've seen Thom naked a couple of times now, but this is the most intimate moment we've had together.

"I need to get back to the concession stand," Thom says. "Go get 'em, tiger."

We bump fists for good luck. I watch him go back through the curtains. I catch Atom's eye after Thom leaves. His face is a mix of envy and concern.

The card begins with the national anthem and the acknowledgement that the event is taking place on First Nations land. Then the announcer starts the show.

"Weighing two hundred pounds from Brooklyn, New York. It's liberal and ironic Brooklyn Tremblay!"

I put on a pair of black-rimmed glasses. I walk past the rows of folding chairs, stopping to take selfies with the Schlepp sisters on my way into the ring. I hop over the top rope and grab the mic from the announcer.

"I hate labels. I don't like having to put everything into little boxes. But if I was going to

TRUE TO YOU

label Golden Adonis, I'd have to call him washed up. Because that's what he's going to be when I'm done with him tonight!"

The audience boos me, all fifty of them. But the Schlepp sisters seem to be enjoying my gimmick.

I drop the mic and go to my corner. I can see Mom and Dad in the audience. Dad is bouncing with excitement. Mom looks nervous. Arshdeep and Pria are sitting with them. I turn around and stretch in the corner. I'm afraid if I look at them too long I'm going to lose my nerve.

"And weighing 230 pounds from Kelowna, B.C., God's gift to wrestling, Golden Adonis!"

The crowd is on its feet. People pat Adonis as he makes his way to the ring. Adonis takes the mic away from the announcer and points to me in my corner.

"Hey, Brooklyn," Adonis says. "How many hipsters does it take to change a light bulb? None. Their mom still does it for them."

I pretend to shout insults back at Adonis. The referee checks us to make sure we don't have anything we can use to hurt each other. Then the bell rings to start the match.

Adonis and I do a variation of the match we did for the student show. We have twenty minutes, so there's plenty of time for a few acrobatic moves off the ropes and outside the ring. The crowd is eating it up. The match ends with me doing a backward moonsault from the top rope. Adonis moves out of the way at the last second. I hear the distinct sound of my mother's shriek in the crowd. I want to give her the thumbs up to let her know I'm okay. But I don't want to spoil the match.

I slowly roll out from under the bottom rope. I pretend to limp back to the dressing area. Romeo and the other wrestlers go wild.

"You nailed it," Romeo says.

"Awesome job," Atom adds. "You looked like a veteran up there."

"Thanks," I reply.

I have to wait out the rest of the show in the changing area. We're not allowed to go back out front until the crowd is nearly gone.

After, I go to meet my parents but I'm stopped by a slap on the back.

"Great match." It's Ricky Flamingo. Ricky is a bottle blond and has a fake tan. His clothes can barely contain all his muscles. "What's your name? Your real name?"

"Jorge."

"Ricky Flamingo. You probably know me from my fed, Lion's Gate Wrestling."

"I've been to a few of your shows," I tell him.

"You looked really good up there," Ricky says. "How long have you been training?"

"Four months," I tell him.

"Impressive," Ricky says. He slips something into my pocket. "Call me."

"Back off, Ricky." Romeo arrives and puts himself in between us. "You're not poaching another one of my superstars."

"I would never do that to you," Ricky says. "Don't need to. I have an impressive group of students myself."

"Cool. Send them to me if they want a real wrestling education."

"Very funny, Romeo. I need to run," Ricky says. He points a finger at me. "I'll keep an eye out for you."

"God, I hate that guy," Romeo says when Ricky's gone.

Mom, Dad, Thom, Arshdeep and Pria all descend on me at the same time.

"What did you think, Mom?" I ask.

"You lost," she said.

"You know the outcomes are pre-determined, right?" I ask her.

"Yeah. I was hoping Romeo would let you win your first match," she says.

"If Jorge keeps getting that kind of response from the crowd, he'll be winning in no time," Romeo says.

Dad puts me in a headlock. Thom gives me a thumbs up. Arshdeep looks happy for me. But I can tell he wishes he was the one getting all this attention.

This was supposed to be his moment. A part of me feels like I stole it from him.

"Do you want your mom and me to drive you home?" Dad asks.

"I was going to help take the ring down. I can get a lift from Thom after he's done cleaning up the concession stand," I say.

"Remember to put ice on anything that hurts before bed," Mom says.

"I will," I tell her.

I put my hand in my pocket as I watch the four of them walk toward the exit. Something pokes my finger. I pull it out. It's Ricky's business card. On the back, he's written, "Let's talk!" followed by his phone number.

12 Poached

"TABLE FOR HOW MANY?" asks the hostess at the White Spot.

I look around the restaurant. Ricky Flamingo is scrolling through his phone at a booth next to the window.

"My friend is already here," I tell her. I knock on the table to let Ricky know I've arrived. "Anybody home?"

"Hey, Jorge!" Ricky gets out of the booth.

He slams his hand into mine like we're old buddies. "Can I order you a beer?"

"I'm underage."

"I doubt the waitress will mind. I think she's hot for me," Ricky says with a wink.

"I'm good."

"Let's get down to business then." Ricky gestures to the bench across from him. "So what are the odds I could lure you to wrestle for LGW?"

"I'd be lying if I said I wasn't interested. But I don't know if I'm ready to cross that bridge yet."

"Then what are you doing here?"

Good question. The last thing I want to do is betray Romeo. But I've never had my ego stroked like this before. No one has ever recognized my talents for anything. Until I started wrestling, people pointed out my shortcomings, not my strengths.

"I understand your obligation to Romeo," Ricky says. "But Romeo knows as much as I do that his fed is a bust. You saw the crowd you wrestled for. You could be playing to a house twice that size."

"I've only had one match," I say. "There's still a lot I need to learn."

"The only way you're going to get better is to wrestle in front of an audience. You were born for this. It shows in the ring."

"Couldn't I wait a few months?"

"This business waits for no one. Remember, there's always someone coming up behind you. You could get injured next week."

"Didn't you hire Thunder after he broke Arshdeep's arm?" I point out.

"Here's my point. Why would you want to headline a wrestling card if no one is there to see you wrestle?" Ricky continues. "Come wrestle for me. I promise to give your career the push it deserves. A year from now, you'll be wrestling Kyle O'Malley for the championship."

Kyle O'Malley. The Holy Grail of indy wrestling. I should have known Ricky would play the Kyle card.

"That is tempting," I say slowly.

"You need to decide what you're worth. Do you

want to spend the next year dragging Romeo's broken ring to Cloverdale? Or do you want to headline a card for a sold-out crowd at the Russian Community Centre here in the city?"

"Can I have a couple of days to think about it?"

"Why don't you come to the next show on the house? Bring a date if you want." An alarm on Ricky's phone goes off. "I have to run. We'll be in touch."

Ricky slides a couple of tickets for the next Lion's Gate show across the table. He puts on a pair of aviator sunglasses and leaves some money for the waitress. I watch him through the window as he walks across the parking lot. He raises his hand and clicks a fob. A big white SUV blinks to life. Ricky gets in and drives away.

I can't help but be starstruck by Ricky. Here's a guy who was just like me not that long ago. Now he's running his own wrestling fed.

"Can I get you anything else?" the waitress asks.

"No thanks," I say.

The waitress takes the money Ricky left for her and walks away.

♥ ♥ ♥

Ricky was right about the size of the crowd at the Lion's Gate Wrestling show. The Russian Community Centre is packed to the gills with marks and hipsters.

"My gimmick would really go over with this crowd," I tell Thom as we find a seat in the balcony.

"Wouldn't they be offended by it?"

"That's how you get heat."

"I'm so sick of that expression," Thom says. I can tell he's annoyed. Which makes me annoyed with him.

Ricky's ring looks brand new. The ring apron doesn't have patches covering up holes. The ropes are all one colour, not held together with electrical tape. There's a big screen flashing graphics and video clips. Four video cameras are aimed at the ring in the centre of the dance floor.

"This is the WWE for a fifth of the budget," I say.

"I thought the WWE was an evil corporation that chews up wrestlers and spits them out."

"Apple uses cheap labour, but you own an iPhone."

Thom raises his eyebrows and looks away. I really should have invited Arshdeep instead of Thom.

The show has a party atmosphere. The crowd gets into the matches, shouting and jeering at the wrestlers. The Schlepp sisters have prime seats near the ring. Some members of the audience are holding up signs. More importantly, they're buying T-shirts and photos at the merchandise table.

And then I see the one person I hoped I would never see again. Thunder runs into the ring to interrupt a match. It's to give the wrestler he's managing an unfair advantage so he can win the match, which the wrestler does. Thunder is wearing a second-hand suit. Ricky is so slick, he can even make Thunder look good.

"Is it me or is every match ending with a low blow or chair across the head?" Thom asks.

"This fed is a little more extreme than Romeo's."

"I noticed that when the whole room started chanting 'fag' during the second match."

"You can't take that seriously. Most of the people aren't that much older than we are. Do you really think they're homophobic?"

"Yes."

For the main event, Ricky defends his title belt against Kyle O'Malley. The crowd goes nuts when Ricky wins with a low blow.

After the show Thom and I drive over to Davie Street. We go to one of the gay restaurants that doesn't require ID.

"So you hated the show," I ask him over dinner.

"Hate is not a family value. But I don't think it's your style."

"You don't think I'm good enough to wrestle for Ricky?"

"I think you're *better* than that. You saw those wrestlers. Most, if not all, of them were on steroids. And the women wrestlers, my God. The only difference between them and strippers was a pole."

"But those wrestlers are working up and down the coast. Some of them are even getting bookings in Japan!"

"And you can't get that wrestling for Romeo?"

"Maybe in about fifty years."

"I think you're being blinded by the bright lights. If you keep working, you are going to get what you want. It's happening. Can't you see that?"

"So I should just keep doing what I'm doing."

"For the time being. If Ricky thinks you're this great prodigy, he's still going to think so a year from now. You're the one with the bargaining chip. He needs you as much you need him."

"And what would you do if I decided to change my allegiance to a different fed?"

"You make it sound like a kingdom in some epic fantasy."

"That's what it is."

"I'll support you any way that I can. But I'm going to say this now in case you get any ideas. I will not tolerate steroids. Also, I'm willing to keep our relationship on the down-low so you can climb the ranks. But I'm not going to put up with blatant homophobia."

"I'm glad you got that off your chest."

"So are you going to go wrestle for Ricky?"

"I still haven't decided," I tell him.

But I had.

13 Betrayal

I CALL ROMEO TO ASK HIM to meet me at the School of Hard Knocks before practice. It takes me forever to reassure him. He thinks I'm in some sort of trouble or got into a fight with my parents. I'm not looking forward to our conversation all the same.

Romeo is making repairs to the ring when I arrive. He looks peaceful and kind of old. He has his headphones on and doesn't hear me come in. I watch him as he finishes taping the top rope. Then he runs back and forth across the ring to test his work. The years fly off his face. I hope I'm in as good shape as he is at his age.

Romeo stops mid-flight when he sees me. I'm still standing at the door.

"Want a quick match on the new canvas?" he asks.

"Sure!"

I love wrestling Romeo. It doesn't matter what hold he puts on me. I barely feel it until he squeezes my arm to signal to reverse the hold. We wrestle for about fifteen minutes, making it up as we go along. Thom was telling me about how jazz players improvise notes when they play. That's it how it feels wrestling Romeo. It's like singing at the top of your lungs without using your voice.

"I needed that," Romeo says after our match. "It's like dancing when no one is watching. I wish I could do it by myself, like masturbating."

"Too much information, Romeo."

"Get over yourself, Jorge. I've seen what you kids look at on the Internet. So what do you need to tell me?"

"I had a meeting with Ricky Flamingo. I'm crossing over to Lion's Gate Wrestling." I can't look Romeo in the face as I say it.

"After all I've done for you?" The look on Romeo's face reminds me of my father's the day I got expelled. "I put my faith in you. And now you're ripping my heart out."

"It's too good a chance to pass up," I explain. "If it wasn't for Arshdeep breaking his arm, it would have been three months before I even made my debut."

"That's not true and you know it! I've treated you like a son!"

"I already have a dad, Romeo. I don't need another one."

"So that's how little you respect me."

"This isn't about you. Maybe I'm thinking about myself."

"I *am* thinking about you, Jorge. Ricky isn't poaching you with your best interests in mind. He's doing it to put me out of business."

"You're always telling us we need to expand our horizons to make a career at this. Now that I am, it's like you're making me feel like a Heel."

"What do you think is going to happen when Ricky finds out you're gay?"

"Who told you I'm gay?"

"I have eyes, Jorge. It's obvious Thom is your boyfriend."

"So what? Thom and I are careful around the marks."

"I think it's great you bring him around. But sooner or later the marks are going to figure it out. That's when you'll need someone in your corner to guide you."

"And you're the only person who can do that?"

"No. But I'm a better friend than Ricky will ever be."

"Plenty of wrestlers have come out of the closet."

"And where are they now? Marks need to believe what goes on in that ring. You destroy that illusion and you're dead in this business."

"I'll cross that bridge when I get to it."

"You have so much talent. Ricky will cut you loose the moment you're of no use to him."

"Stop trying to scare me, Romeo. This is hard enough as it is."

"Get out!" Romeo says. His pain turns to anger and he slams his fist on the canvas. "I can't look at you right now."

"Romeo, come on."

"I'm serious. I'm done with you."

I do as he says before he starts talking with his fists.

My phone rings as I'm driving home. Arshdeep's pic appears on my screen. I turn on the hands-free device so I can talk and drive.

"Dude! What the hell did you say to Romeo? He cancelled practice as soon as we got there. I've never seen him so angry."

I was hoping I would have a couple of hours to

myself before I told Arshdeep. Screw it. I might as well piss off all my friends at once.

"Ricky Flamingo asked me to wrestle for Lion's Gate. I said yes."

"When?"

"A week ago. Sorry I didn't tell you sooner. But everything happened so fast."

"I'd be lying if I said I wasn't jealous. But let's face it, you have a better shot of getting discovered working for Ricky."

"This should have been your shot, man."

"Don't blame yourself. Blame Thunder. He's the one who broke my arm."

"You know what sucks? This is the best thing that ever happened. But Romeo is making me out to be a jerk."

"I think you're doing the right thing."

"Honestly?"

"Sikh's honour. Just remember to put in a good word for me with Ricky when the time comes. But don't tell Romeo I said that."

"Don't worry. I don't think I'll be talking to Romeo again."

"Give him time. What does Thom think about you switching feds?"

"I haven't told him yet. I took him to one of Ricky's shows and he wasn't too keen on it."

"You don't want to keep it from him for too long. That's the sort of thing that ends relationships."

"I'll do it tonight. I promise."

"Take it easy, buddy. I'm around if you need me."

I turn off the phone. I feel slightly better than when I left the School of Hard Knocks. I should be soaring off the top rope. But instead it feels like a low blow.

Dad is smoking behind the store when I get home. It's starting to feel like summer. Dad has his face to the sun, enjoying the warmth.

"I thought you had wrestling practice today," Dad says as I get out of the car.

"So did I," I tell him. "Romeo kicked me out of the school."

"You told him about Lion's Gate then."

"Yeah. It didn't go so well. I thought I might be able to reason with him. But he hates Ricky too much."

"Can't say I blame him. There's nothing worse than a snotnose kid moving in on your business. They think they know everything."

"Dad, *I'm* a snotnose kid."

"But you don't act like life started when the iPhone was invented."

"Do you think I'm making the right decision?"

"What I think has nothing to do with it."

"You're the only person who has supported me in my wrestling career. I need to know what you think."

Dad grinds his cigarette out with his foot. "Well, you asked," he says. "I wish you had stuck it out with Romeo a little longer. He wants the best for you. This Ricky character is all show, no soul. Something tells me he'll sweep you under the rug as soon as he's done with you."

"That's what Romeo said. Did he tell you to say that?"

"Great minds just think alike."

"I didn't mean to disappoint you."

"Jorge, I have watched you struggle your whole life. You have no idea how happy it makes your mom and me to see you come into your own."

"That makes this all worthwhile."

"Have you told Thom yet?"

"Why are you and Arshdeep worried about what Thom thinks?"

"Maybe because we think he's good for you. We don't want you guys to break up."

"I've been avoiding telling Thom. He doesn't think much of Ricky and his fed either."

"Don't wait too long."

"That's what Arshdeep said."

"I'm two for two today. I should buy a lottery ticket."

Dad walks back into the shop, leaving me alone in the parking lot. I pull out my phone and dial Thom's number.

14 Looking the Part

THE LION'S GATE WRESTLING GYM is in what used to be a karate studio. Unlike the School of Hard Knocks, it looks like a real gym. It has treadmills and universal weights, as well as free weights. There's even a sponge pit where you can practise aerial moves. One whole wall is nothing but mirrors so you can watch yourself in the ring.

I try not to look too awestruck when I see the space. The place must cost a fortune to run. Granted,

Ricky charges double what Romeo does, though Romeo has the reputation for being a better trainer.

"Welcome to the big leagues, buddy!" Ricky says to me.

A half dozen wrestlers are getting ready for practice. I recognize a couple of the guys and girls from the show I saw with Thom. There's also novice wrestlers who are clearly still learning the ropes.

Some of the wrestlers look at me with suspicion. I feel like I've just walked in on them talking about me.

"I was just showing the gang the *Sweat and Blood Blog*," Ricky says. He hands me his tablet for me to see Bobby's latest post. "You're front page news, kid."

The headline reads: *Brooklyn Tremblay latest superstar acquired by Lion's Gate!* The blog describes my impressive debut with Canadian Pacific Wrestling Federation. It mentions that I have been trained by none other than Romeo Stallone. The blogger goes on to wonder how long CPW can survive if Ricky keeps poaching Romeo's talent.

Great, I think. *Let's add insult to injury.*

"How did Bobby Bentley find out so soon I left CPW?" I ask.

"A little bird told him."

I get a sinking feeling in my stomach. I know Ricky's actions are purely selfish. But I didn't think he would stoop to rubbing this in Romeo's face. Who am I kidding? Pro wrestling is all about rubbing someone's failure in their face.

This was not how I wanted to start my career at Lion's Gate. My head start in the fed is going to piss off some of the other wrestlers. This will likely make them hate me more.

"You can start practice! I'm here now!" a voice shouts.

I turn to see Thunder enter the gym. He stops dead in his tracks when he sees me with Ricky.

"What are *you* doing here?" he asks me.

"Don't you read the Internet?" Ricky asks him. "Brooklyn is the latest addition to my stable."

Thunder's face goes cold. I wish Arshdeep was here to see it.

Practice goes smoothly. I'm a little nervous. But I quickly adapt to everyone's style. I make a connection with Jamie, one of the girl wrestlers. We have great chemistry in the ring.

Halfway through practice Kyle O'Malley shows up to work out. Everyone stops when he enters. It's like John Cena has graced us with his presence. All eyes are on Kyle. Everyone wants to impress him.

After we finish our drills, I work with a couple of the mid-level wrestlers on new moves. I decide to be their punching bag, hoping to win them over. It works. After about thirty minutes, they let me try out some moves of my own.

Ricky and Kyle O'Malley greet me when I climb out of the ring.

"Good work tonight," Ricky says. "Have you met Kyle O'Malley?"

"Not yet. I'm a big fan," I say, shaking Kyle's hand.

"Ricky has been raving about you since he saw your debut," says Kyle. "You're really smooth up there."

"That means a lot coming from you," I say humbly.

"Can I give you a piece of advice, though? You might want to consider taking supplements."

"Supplements?"

"Steroids. You look like a little kid against some of those guys."

"I couldn't have said it better myself," Ricky cuts in. "You have the moves of a star. But you have the body of a teenager."

I flash back to my talk with Thom after the show at the Russian Community Centre. He said he wouldn't tolerate steroids. But would he still feel that way after I get all cut and muscly?

"It's just an idea," Kyle says. "But you'll start getting bookings in the States if you pump up. I know from experience."

"Think about it, Jorge," Ricky says, slapping my shoulder.

Somehow, when Ricky tells you to think about something, you know he's telling you to do it.

A couple of nights later, Thom and I are on a double-date with Arshdeep and Pria. The four of us are celebrating the removal of Arshdeep's cast. His doctor told him he can't wrestle for another couple of weeks. But at least now he can start working out with light weights.

We go out to dinner and then a movie. Thom and Pria act like Arshdeep and I aren't even there. Watching them together, you would think they were dating each other.

We find our seats in the movie theatre. I say, "I'm going to get some snacks."

"I thought you aren't eating junk food," Thom says.

"Popcorn doesn't have any calories," I say.

"Movie theatre popcorn does. You can taste the yellow dye and edible oil product in your mouth," Pria says.

"I'll do an extra an hour of cardio this week."

"I'll come with you then," Thom says.

"It's okay," I say. "You stay here and catch up with Pria."

"Can you get me Red Vines and a 7-Up?" he asks.

"Want to come, Arshdeep?" I ask. I hope this doesn't turn into a scene.

"Can you get me popcorn, sweetie?" Pria asks him, petting his arm like it's a cat.

"See you what you started?" Arshdeep says to me.

As soon as we're out in the lobby, I grab Arshdeep by the arm and pull him off to the side.

"Easy, bro!" he says. "That arm just came out of a cast."

"Sorry. But I've needed to talk to you alone all night."

"What's up?"

I tell Arshdeep about meeting Kyle O'Malley. I tell him about his suggestion that I do steroids.

"What do you think, Arshdeep?" I ask.

"I knew that guy had to be on something. He bulked up way too fast."

"So what do you think?"

"You're not seriously asking my permission to do steroids, are you?"

"We both know the guys who get booked out of province look like gladiators."

"There are plenty of guys our size doing well."

"I just want to fit in at Lion's Gate. I feel weird getting a push in the fed after only one match."

"Steroids are a slippery slope, bro. Have you noticed that most of the WWE wrestlers who died young were doing steroids?"

"I won't be on them forever. Just to get a quick start."

"What does Thom think?"

"He said before that he wouldn't tolerate steroids."

"Then there's your answer."

"He probably won't even notice. I work out tons already."

"Steroids don't just give you muscles, Jorge. You're going to get zits on your back. And your balls are going to shrink."

"What?"

"Once your balls stop making hormones, they shrink."

"Forever?"

"That's not the point. The point is that it isn't something you can hide from Thom. And I don't want you screwing things up with him. I like the guy. And not just because he amuses Pria."

"He got over my leaving Canadian Pacific Wrestling. I'm sure he won't mind once he can bounce a dime off my stomach."

"What about 'roid rage?"

"I'll do yoga."

"You sound like you've already made up your mind about this."

"It's not like I haven't thought about it before."

"You're playing with fire, bro. If this blows up in your face, you can't say I didn't warn you."

My phone vibrates inside my pocket. It's Thom letting me know the trailers are starting.

"Come on," I say. "Let's go to the snack bar before Thom and Pria come looking for us."

"It's not Pria I'm worried about."

15 Old Wounds

MY BODY IS KILLING ME when I wake up for my shift at the store. I crawl out of bed and take a couple of Advil then turn on the shower as hot as it will go. The heat feels good on my back. What I really need is a massage.

I've been doing steroids for a couple of weeks now. Only Arshdeep and Ricky Flamingo know I'm taking them. Ricky is my supplier as well. I've yet to see any difference in the size of my muscles. Ricky says it will take a month before I see results.

The worst part about doing steroids (besides the cost) is the injections. I have to keep the needles out of my parent's sight. I don't want them thinking I'm taking heroin. Not that steroids would make them feel any better.

I've also been having a hard time controlling my temper, especially during practice. Thunder has been doing his best to get under my skin. I've learned to count to one hundred before I respond to his taunts. Still, there are times when I see some guy acting like a douchebag in public and I want to get in his face.

The best part about steroids is all the energy I have. I can work out way longer at the gym. I'm lifting heavier weights. My progress has caused a bit of tension between Arshdeep and myself. He's been trying to add muscle naturally for a while now. Whenever I brag about how much weight I'm lifting he reminds me I'm on steroids. He tries to pass it off as a joke. But I get the sense he's not kidding.

I find I have more endurance in the ring.

I can take harder bumps and fight more aggressively. Taking steroids has also helped me bond with some of the better wrestlers at Lion's Gate. If I keep up the pace, I should be headlining an event any month now.

I get dressed and head down to the store. I find Thom standing by the counter with a bouquet of flowers. Mom and Dad are grinning from ear to ear.

"Surprise!" Mom, Dad and Thom say.

"What's going on?" I ask, still half asleep.

"It's our six-month anniversary!" Thom says. "Don't tell me you forgot."

"Of course he did," Mom says. "He forgets my birthday every year."

"I'm confused," I say. "I thought Dad needed me to work today."

"Your mom and I have been planning this surprise for a week now," says Thom.

"Someone get this kid a cup of coffee," Dad says.

Mom makes me a double-espresso. I go outside with Thom and drink it on the patio.

"So what do you want to do?" I ask.

"I have it all planned. We can rent a tandem bike and ride the Seawall. Then I booked us a couple's massage at a spa."

"Tandem bike? You mean one of those bikes two people ride at once?"

"Do you mind? I've always thought they were romantic."

"Not at all. I feel bad because I didn't get you a card or anything."

"You can repay me later." Thom winks at me.

"I have the best boyfriend in the world," I say. Now I feel even more guilty about the secrets I'm keeping.

I've never ridden a bicycle for two before. Neither has Thom. It takes a few stops and starts before we get the hang of it. We nearly fall over once, but manage to catch ourselves at the last second.

I'm in front, controlling our speed and direction. I was in way better shape than Thom before. Now I'm on steroids. I have to remember my own strength or we're going to get hurt.

It's a beautiful day. There are tourists and families on the Seawall so we have to take our time. We have to watch out for the little kids who are still wobbling on their tiny bikes.

"We should invite Arshdeep and Pria to do this sometime," Thom says as we ride past the expensive condos in Coal Harbour.

"You really like Pria, don't you?"

"She's sassy. She's like an Indian Rhianna."

"It's nice to have another couple we can hang out with. The four of us balance each other out."

"Would you smell that fresh air? Can you believe they want to pollute this with more tankers?"

"Can we not talk about politics today?"

"You can't hide from the universe, Jorge." We ride in silence until we get to Prospect Point. Behind us I hear some guys on roller blades swearing up a storm. I feel my shoulders tense up. I know that voice. I turn around and see Ian Adamson. He's the guy I fought with the day I was expelled from school. He and his crew are up to their old tricks, making life miserable for everyone.

"Fags!" Ian shouts, as he whips by us.

I stand up on the pedals and get set to take off after him.

"Settle down!" Thom says to me. "They're just assholes. Nothing you do or say is going to change that."

I start to count down from one hundred. When I get to ninety I see Ian cut off a little kid on his bike. The kid falls over and starts crying. The kid's parents stop to make sure he's okay.

Screw it.

I put all my weight on the pedals and take off after Ian and his pals. They have a hundred metres on us but a slope on the bike path helps us gain on them. Ian sees that we're on their tail. All of them take off as fast as they can.

"Jorge! Stop! I can't keep up!" Thom shouts.

I wish I could ditch Thom so I could go faster. We're starting to gain on them. I cut across onto the pedestrian path. A jogger shouts at us when I cut him off. Ian is less than ten metres ahead of us. If I can just push myself a little harder . . .

"Jorge! You're scaring me!"

Thom's words hit me like a ton of bricks. I stop pedalling until it's safe to put the brakes on the bike. Ian looks back and sees that we've given up the chase. He gives me the finger and disappears around the next bend in the Seawall.

Thom and I get off the bike. We walk it to the side of the Seawall out of the other cyclists' way. A few more joggers give us what for as they go by.

"What is wrong with you?" Thom asks. "This is our anniversary, not some stupid grudge match!" He leaves the bike and walks ahead of me toward a bench. I try to keep up with him, but the bike is awkward for one person to push.

"Thom, wait!" I say. "I didn't mean to lose my

temper. I know that guy from school. I got expelled because of him."

"Is that supposed to make me feel better?" Thom puts his face in his hands and starts to cry.

"Thom, please don't cry. People are starting to stare."

"Let me get this straight. It's okay for you to act like a homicidal maniac. But I can't be upset that you nearly got us killed on a tandem bike."

"You're being dramatic."

"I took my feet off the pedals. You were going so fast!"

"But I stopped before things got out of control."

"I don't believe you. I went out of my way to make this day special for both of us. You've ruined it. And not just today. I've never seen anyone get that angry before. What if you ever get that mad at me?"

"You know I would never hurt you."

"That's what abusive boyfriends say."

"Thom, look at me."

He lifts his face and wipes away the tears.

I tell him, "I could never live with myself if I did anything to hurt you."

Thom looks confused. I can see him debating what to do next. I can't say I blame him.

"I think I should just go home," he finally says.

16 Thin Ice

GETTING BACK INTO THOM'S good graces is not easy. It takes a week of begging, flowers and dinners at restaurants. I even convince him to come with me to Ricky's birthday party.

Everybody who is anybody in B.C. indy wrestling circles is going to be there. I don't really want to go, but I promised Arshdeep I would get him there so he could have face time with Ricky. Arshdeep is still a long way from peak shape, but he wants Ricky to be aware of him for when he is.

"I have bad news," Thom says when he arrives to pick me up for the party. Thom points to his car parked behind the store. Lionel is sitting in the front seat, his head against the passenger window.

"What's he doing here?" I ask.

"Eddy dumped him. He showed up on my doorstep, drunk and depressed."

"We can't take him to the party."

"I can't just leave him in my car."

"Why not? He's not your boyfriend anymore."

"He's still my friend."

"Fine. But you have to keep an eye on him. I'm going to this party as a favour to Arshdeep. I don't need any gay drama."

"Do you want to go alone?"

"I'm sorry. I'm stressed. This party is a really big deal and I'm afraid of doing something stupid."

"You're already on thin ice, mister."

Arshdeep is waiting for us in his car when we get to Ricky's house. Pria is with him.

"Why aren't you inside?" I ask him, getting out of Thom's car.

"I was waiting for you!" Arshdeep says. "I don't know any of these people."

"That's the whole point of inviting you to the party."

"Hey, babe!" Pria gives Thom a big hug.

"Hey, girl!" Thom says.

"Who's that guy?" Arshdeep asks when he sees Lionel.

"Arshdeep, Pria, this my ex-boyfriend, Lionel," Thom says.

"In spite of my current condition I'm very pleased to meet you," Lionel says. He looks like he's trying not to throw up.

"Let's just get this over with," I say.

"That's the party spirit," Pria says. She minces across the driveway in her high heels.

The party is in full swing. I didn't get invited to

parties when I was in school, so the number of people crowded into Ricky's living room overwhelms me. I grab the back of Thom's shirt before we get too far into the house.

"What's wrong?" Thom asks.

"There's so many people. And this house is a mansion." I can feel myself starting to freak out.

"It's just a house. Take a deep breath. Smile and be yourself."

"I don't know how to do that."

"Then pretend everyone you meet is me."

I lean against the wall. I take deep breaths until I feel normal again.

"I'm sorry I've been such a horrible boyfriend lately," I say to Thom.

"Dating is hard, Jorge. If we can't learn to weather the rough patches how are we going to enjoy the good times?"

"I want to kiss you so bad."

"Not now. That wrestling blogger is here." Thom gestures to where Bobby Bentley is talking to Thunder.

"That guy is everywhere," I say.

"Crap! I lost Lionel," says Thom. "Go find Arshdeep and Pria. I'll catch up with you."

I find Pria alone in the kitchen holding a red plastic cup. She does not look impressed.

"Where's Arshdeep?" I ask her.

"Off talking to one of his wrestling bros. Where's Thom?"

"Looking for Lionel."

"Good. Now I can give you a piece of my mind. What the hell was that stunt you pulled in Stanley Park?"

"When did Thom tell you about that? I haven't even told Arshdeep."

"Hello! Thom and I talk, text and Snapchat daily. Get over it."

"It's none of your business, Pria. No one got hurt."

"This time! What are you doing? Do you have any idea what you have in Thom? He is like a black Beyoncé!"

"Beyoncé *is* black."

"Don't interrupt me! So help me, if you hurt

Thom I will come after you like the goddess Durga, eight arms a-swinging. Do you hear me?"

"I hear you. I care for him more than you know."

"Jorge!" someone shouts into my ear. I stagger under the sudden weight of Ricky Flamingo. He is well on his way to being piss drunk. "Who's this? Your girlfriend?" he asks.

"Ha!" Pria says.

"This is my friend, Pria," I say. "She's dating a friend of mine I want to introduce to you. There he is now." I wave my hand over the crowd to get Arshdeep's attention. He heads toward us as soon as he sees I'm with Ricky. "Ricky, this is my buddy, Arshdeep. We trained together at the School of Hard Knocks."

Ricky takes a closer look at Arshdeep's face. "I know you! You broke Thunder's arm."

"It was the other way around," Arshdeep corrects him.

"That's right. I've heard good things about you from Bobby Bentley. You wrestling again yet?"

"Just got my cast off."

"Congratulations. I'll keep an eye out for you. Who knows, maybe I can lure you to Lion's Gate in the future."

"That would be awesome."

"I need a drink!" Ricky shouts. He staggers away.

"Can we leave now?" I say after Ricky is gone.

"Our work here is done," says Arshdeep.

"You two stay here," I tell them. "I'm going to look for Thom and Lionel." I turn around and walk right into Thunder. His drink spills all over his cheap nylon shirt.

"Watch it, dick!" Thunder says. His face freezes when he sees who we are. "Arshdeep. How's the arm?"

"Better. No thanks to you."

"Accidents happen," Thunder snarls.

"Especially when you're in the ring," says Pria.

"Who's that dude you were with earlier, Jorge?" Thunder says to me. "Your boyfriend?"

"And if it was?" I say.

"You want to be careful," Thunder taunts me.

"Bobby Bentley is here. You know how he likes to gossip in his blog."

"Someone should tell him how you broke Arshdeep's arm," I fire back.

"Yeah?" Thunder gets in my face.

"Yeah!" I meet his gaze.

"Jorge! What were you and I just talking about?" Pria says.

"Ignore him, Jorge," Arshdeep says. "He's just trying to screw up your career. Just like he did mine."

I don't even need to count to one hundred. I go off to look for Thom and Lionel.

The party is even busier than when we arrived. I'm dripping sweat as I squeeze through the halls and make my way upstairs. There's a long line for the bathroom. For a brief second I worry that Thom and Lionel are in there making out.

I see a door open just a crack at the end of the hall. I push it open to look inside, hoping I don't catch anyone having sex. Instead I find Lionel sitting next to Bobby Bentley on a bed.

"Lionel! Time to go!" I say.

"Hey, Jorge! Have you met Bobby?" Lionel is clearly having the time of his life. It must be hair of the dog.

"Hey, Bobby!" I say. "I hope Lionel hasn't been harassing you."

"Not at all," Bobby says.

I help Lionel to his feet and lead him back down the hall.

"That guy was so into me," Lionel says.

"I bet."

"Oh, and by the way. I'm going to break up you and Thom. I'm getting him back if it's the last thing I do."

I look to see if Lionel is kidding. He's not smiling.

"You can do that as soon as we get out of here," I say.

Arshdeep and Pria are where I left them. Thom is with them too.

"Where the hell were you?" Thom asks Lionel.

"Don't ask. Let's just go," I answer for him. "I've had enough fun for one night."

17 *Outed*

I'M REALLY EXCITED ABOUT practice tonight. Ricky is planning on announcing the card for the next show. I'm hoping he puts me up against one of the mid-level wrestlers instead of a student near the bottom of the card. At the same time, I don't want to be too near the top of the card. That would create friction with the other wrestlers. I really don't need that right now.

I have half an hour to spare, so I kill time

watching matches on YouTube. Then I click on Bobby Bentley's wrestling blog, *Sweat and Blood*, to see if there's something about my upcoming debut for Lion's Gate Wrestling. My jaw drops when I see the headline for the latest blog post:

Lion's Gate Wrestling's Newest Addition is Gay!

What the hell?

This weekend I learned that Brooklyn Tremblay, Lion's Gate Wrestling's newest star, is gay and has a boyfriend.

The question is, will Brooklyn use his sexuality in his gimmick? And if he does, what impact will it have on his career?

There have been rumours that a prominent veteran wrestler has been in a gay relationship for twenty years. But he denied it when I asked him about it.

I think it would be great to have an openly gay wrestler working the circuit. It's about time pro wrestling caught up with the rest of the world.

I nearly lose my head the first time I read the post. Then I go back and read it again. I realize it's a pretty positive piece. It makes me wonder if Lionel was right and Bobby is gay. There is no doubt in my mind that Lionel is the one who outed me to Bobby.

I scroll to the bottom of the blog post and start reading the comments.

Fag!

I'll stop going to LGW shows if that homo is wrestling.

He better hire some security to keep him safe from me.

For all I know, the comments are from some troll in his underwear sitting in his parents' basement. Most of the marks at the shows are harmless. They use the action in the ring to get out their aggression. It makes me nervous all the same. What if someone figures out what Thom looks like and takes it out on him?

I consider skipping practice. But the other wrestlers would think I'm ashamed of being gay. If there's one thing I'm not, it's ashamed of who I am. I have Thom to thank for that. I sling my gym bag over my shoulder, stick out my chest and head to practice.

To my surprise, the other wrestlers are supportive.

"My brother is gay," says Sauron, the Masked Man. "If anyone screws with you, I've got your back."

"Thanks!" I tell him.

"Don't let those idiots get to you," Jamie tells me. "I'm gay and I'm as tough as they come."

"Why aren't you out then?" I ask her. Jamie is the women's champion. Why would she need to keep it secret?

"I'm sure the marks are already thinking about me having sex with my opponents," she says.

That's not what I call gay pride. But I'm not going to knock it.

The only person who is enjoying my misery is Thunder.

"I knew you were gay from the moment you started training!" Thunder says, showing up for practice late.

"It takes one to know one," I tell him.

"I'm as straight as they come."

"That's what closet cases tell themselves."

"Just don't give me AIDS in the ring," Thunder says.

I start to lose my temper and move in on Thunder. Jamie stops me before I do anything stupid.

"Thunder, if I find it was you who outed me to Bobby, I'm going to pile drive you for real," I tell him.

"Save the trash talk for the ring, Jorge," Ricky says. "I think you need a quick timeout. Why don't we go for a walk on the treadmill?" He turns and says, "The rest of you get warmed up."

I follow Ricky to the cardio area. We each get on a treadmill and start walking like we're outside.

I guess I should start. "Ricky, I'm sorry I didn't tell you I was gay. I didn't know how everyone would react."

"We're monsters in the ring, not in real life, Jorge. But I realize it's not easy coming out. Especially in this business."

"Tell me about it."

"It's not the end of the world though. I think I know how we can make this work."

"Can't we just ignore it? What I do in private isn't anybody's business."

"You're forgetting an important point. You are your gimmick in and out of the ring. When the marks see you in street clothes, they don't see Jorge, they see Brooklyn Tremblay."

"So what do I do?"

"Play it up. Instead of burying it, I say we shove your gayness in the marks' faces."

"Like Gorgeous George and Adrian Street? But isn't that playing into people's homophobia?"

"That's pro wrestling."

"I can't do that. Even if I was straight, I couldn't do that."

"I'm sorry to hear that, Jorge," says Ricky.

"Because if you don't make the most of this chance to get some heat, you won't be wrestling for Lion's Gate."

I flash back to my talk with Romeo. He saw this coming a mile away. I didn't listen.

"If it makes you feel any better," Ricky goes on, "you can debut the gimmick on Thunder. I'll let you squash him. If he so much as puts up a fight, I'll let you beat him up for real."

That does sweeten the deal. But it doesn't make me feel any better about the gimmick.

I drive out to see Thom after practice. I tell him about the blog post. But I leave out Ricky's idea for the gimmick.

"This is good news!" Thom says. "Now we don't have to sneak around when we're with your wrestling buddies."

I should have known he would think that. Thom doesn't get pro wrestling at all.

"You should read the comments on the blog post," I say. "I've never felt so hated in all my life."

"A lot of people hate gay people. You better get used to it no matter what you end up doing."

Thom still thinks wrestling is just a hobby for me. He sounds like his father.

"Why couldn't this have happened after I proved myself in the ring?" I moan. "This wouldn't be so bad if I had a fan base."

"People will forget about this. It's not the eighties. Maybe you'll pave the way for more gay wrestlers to come out."

"I don't want to be a figurehead. I just want to wrestle."

"Gay people don't always get that option. Try being black and gay."

I know Thom is trying to help. But I really wish he wouldn't bring the conversation back to himself. For once I wish I could just vent without being interrupted.

"This is all Lionel's fault," I say.

"What?"

"He was talking to Bobby Bentley at the party."

"You're being paranoid."

"So Lionel gets the benefit of the doubt and I don't?"

"Lionel would never out another gay guy. It's not his style."

"Could have fooled me. And I didn't tell you this, but Lionel vowed to break us up."

"That's it. I've had it. You have to go."

"So, let me get this straight. The minute I point out something that bugs me about you, it's conversation closed."

"I think we need a little time apart to think about this relationship."

"You're breaking up with me?"

"No. But if you don't go, I might."

Man, life is just like wrestling, the good guys can't catch a break.

18 Heel Turn

I HAVEN'T SEEN THOM in the week since our argument. We've texted back and forth a bit. But he's still pretty upset that I accused Lionel of outing me.

Part of me feels that Thom is being too dramatic. But mostly I'm worried that our relationship is over. Thom and I have had our ups and downs, but he's made me really think about my future. I can't help but wonder if I shouldn't have taken his advice more.

I'm glad that Thom won't be at the Russian Community Centre to see me debut my new "Big Gay Hipster" gimmick. I still hate the idea, but I promised Ricky I would try it out. I don't have much of a choice. He made it clear: "My way or the highway."

The time comes for the ring announcer to introduce my match with Thunder. I make my way to the ring as usual. I stop to take a selfie with the Schlepp sisters. One of them pushes me away. The other spits at me. I know this is part of the show but it's hard not to take it personally.

I take my corner in the ring. There are catcalls of "fag" and "fudge packer" from the crowd. Ricky and the other wrestlers prepared me for this at our last practice. I know the other wrestlers are ready to pounce if things get ugly. I hope it doesn't come to that.

Thunder's entrance is met with boos and jeers. He tries to quiet the crowd so he can insult me on the mic.

The crowd is having none of it. They hate Thunder. But the marks who have read Bobby's blog hate me even more.

"Kill that pansy!" someone shouts above the crowd.

The announcer looks at me like she's worried for my life. She gets out of the ring as fast as she can.

The bell rings. Thunder and I circle, sizing up each other. I put Thunder in a headlock. A couple of Thunder's gut punches actually connect with my stomach. I block his next punch and push him into the ropes. I slap my hand across his chest so hard it leaves a red mark.

"Quit it," I whisper into his ear. "I'm on steroids. You don't want to make me angry." Then I whip him off the ropes and flip him over my back.

It's almost time for me to play the gay card. Once I go gay, there's no going back. This is either going to boost my career or kill it right here.

Romeo's voice drifts through my mind. "Remember to tell a story when you're wrestling."

I decide this match is the story of a guy being forced into a box he didn't create. It's a story about being open to possibilities, but being judged by people who can't see past their noses.

I push Thunder into the corner and kiss him on the lips.

This wasn't in our practice match at the gym. Thunder pushes me away and wipes his face like I just gave him cooties. The crowd is on its feet. No one can believe what just happened.

For the rest of the match, everything I do has a sexual overtone. The crowd is eating it up. To my surprise, I am too. I start to feed off their hatred. It informs every hold I apply, every move I make. Thunder is at a loss to stay in the match. I'm completely upstaging him. I set up the end of the match with a low blow and get ready for my big finish.

Will Thunder stay in position when I go for the moonsault? I climb to the top turnbuckle and give the marks the finger. Some of them throw stuff at me. It feels amazing. Then I do a backflip and land across

Thunder's chest. I straddle him for the pin and the crowd goes nuts.

When I get backstage, Ricky is excited. "That was insane!" he says. "Keep that up and you'll be wrestling Kyle O'Malley by the end of the year."

"Really?" I ask.

"You need to start selling some merchandise," Ricky says. "People are going to want a piece of you."

I help the crew take down the ring even though I don't have to. I don't want anyone thinking I have a big head. A few of the wrestlers invite me to join them for something to eat at the Cactus Club to celebrate. I tell them I'll meet them there.

To my surprise, Thom is waiting for me at the van. I'm so glad to see him, I open my arms for a hug. Then I see the look on his face.

"What the hell was that supposed to be?" he asks. I've never seen him so angry.

"It's my new gimmick. Did you see how the crowd ate it up?"

"That was the most disgusting thing I've seen in my life."

"It wasn't that bad."

"Are you on crack? Oh, of course not . . . you're on steroids. No one gets that big that fast."

"I need to look the part to make it in this business."

"That day in the park makes so much sense to me now."

"Can we go somewhere and talk about this calmly?"

"We are beyond that now. I actually came here ready to apologize. But after what you did in there I'm embarrassed to be seen with you. We're over."

Thom turns his back on me and gets into his car. I bang on the window to get him to roll it down. But he leaves me in his dust.

I was so upset I didn't hear the metal stage door open and close behind me. It's not until I turn around that I realize Thunder and the other wrestlers have seen the whole fight.

"Aww . . . did the flamer break up with his boyfriend?" Thunder says. He looks and sounds like Ian Adamson.

Without thinking, I drop my gym bag and charge toward him. Thunder starts to run but I'm too fast. I can hear the other wrestlers yelling for me to stop, but I don't care. I grab Thunder by the back of his coat and spin him around. I can see the fear in his eyes as I pull back my arm and punch him in the face.

Thunder hits the ground like a bag of cement. He's not moving. My heart starts to race. Jamie runs to his side to see if he's breathing.

"Call 911!" she shouts to the other wrestlers.

I start to panic. I want to run. But that will only make it worse. It's finally happened. I let my temper get the best of me. I've done something I can't take back.

19 Below the Belt

RICKY DOESN'T WASTE ANY TIME kicking me out of Lion's Gate Wrestling.

"I don't blame you for punching Thunder," he says on the phone. "But he has a restraining order on you. I can't have you anywhere near him."

"Why don't you kick *him* out of the fed? I'm the draw, not Thunder."

"I thought about that. But word gets around fast. I can't risk you going off on another wrestler.

It's bad for business."

I want to go off on Ricky. The only reason I lost control is because the steroids he was supplying me with were screwing with my hormones. But I have no one to blame but myself. Romeo, Dad and Thom warned me about Ricky. Now I'm paying the price.

The only friends I have left are my parents and Arshdeep. Arshdeep and I hang out. But I'm jealous that he's still able to pursue his dream while I'm stuck stocking the shelves at the store.

My head is clearer since I stopped taking the steroids. I replay the last few months over in my mind. For all my success in the ring, I realize something. All the highlights involved Thom: the protest, the day on Burnaby Mountain and all those quiet times in between.

For six months, people were praising my ability in the ring. But Thom was the only one who saw me for who I am. He listened to me when I was scared. He calmed me down when I was angry. He even kept my hands from shaking before my debut match. I can't believe I put wrestling before him.

I'm dying to tell Thom I'm sorry. But he won't answer my calls or return my texts. I want to hear his voice again, even if it's yelling at me. I need to hear him get what he has to say off his chest. So I do the next best thing.

"What do you want?" Pria says coldly into the phone.

"Advice. How do I make things right with Thom?"

"You can't."

"I don't believe you."

"You have an assault charge hanging over your head, Jorge. That is not attractive."

"So am I just supposed to curl up into a ball and die?"

"It's a start."

"I've thought about it."

"Ugh. You and Arshdeep are exactly alike. You project this tough image when all you really want is a hug."

"I admit that I screwed up. I can't even pretend to makes excuses for how I behaved. But I can't let go of Thom without a fight."

"This isn't a wrestling match, Jorge. Fighting won't get Thom back."

"So what do I do?"

"You make peace with yourself. That's the only way Thom is ever going to be able to look you in the eye again. You need to remind him of the guy he had feelings for."

"How do I do that?"

"Who am I, the goddess Parvathi?"

"Who's she?"

"Google her." Pria takes a breath. "Maybe you can volunteer at a soup kitchen or sign up to become a Big Brother. I wish I could give you a five-point plan to solve all your problems. But I can't. Whatever you do, you have to accept that Thom might never want to talk to you again."

"That's what I'm afraid of."

"I wish I could be more help. I know I can

be really rough on you, but only because I actually like you."

"At least someone does."

I spend a few days reading a book my mom bought: *The Power of Now: A Guide to Spiritual Enlightenment.*

"Oprah swears by it," Mom says.

I've been doing yoga at the community centre. I downloaded a meditation app for my phone. Mom thinks I should start going to church again, but I'm not ready take the Jesus route to inner peace.

Yoga and meditating help, but I still find myself getting angry if I'm not careful. Yesterday some guy on his cell phone tried to butt in line in front of Mrs. Lopez. She is like a hundred years old. I almost lost it on him.

Today on my break at the store, I am flipping through the *The Province* and see Thom's photo. It's next to an article he wrote: "Clean Air and Water:

My Future depends on it".

I hug the newspaper to my chest. I'm so proud of him. I want to call him and congratulate him on getting in the paper. But I know he won't take my call.

I go to a yoga class after my shift at the store. I try to clear my head with my breath but it isn't working. I keep looking at the clock. I'm counting the minutes until class is over and I can drive to Thom's house in Surrey. I need to talk to him in person.

For our final yoga pose, we sit cross-legged with our hands resting on our knees. An image of Pria appears in my head. She has eight arms. All eight of her index fingers are waving at me, warning me against doing what I'm thinking of doing.

Imaginary Pria is right. Seeing Thom will just make things worse. But then crazy wrestler Jorge takes Pria's place and says, "What's the harm in congratulating someone for a job well done?"

It's just after seven o'clock when I get to Thom's house. I can either wait in my car for Thom to come out, or knock on the door. If one of his parents answers, I'll get the door slammed in my face. As I ponder my options, I realize what I'm doing is crazy. It doesn't stop me from getting out of the car and ringing Thom's doorbell.

Thom opens the door. "Jorge," he says. "What are you doing here?"

"I saw your article in the paper today."

"You shouldn't be here." Thom starts to close the door. I stop it with my hand.

"Can't we just talk?" I ask.

"Please take your hand off my door. You're scaring me."

"Don't be like this." I worry that I'm going to start to cry.

"I don't know what you think you're doing. But from where I'm standing, this looks like stalking."

My mind starts to spin. Why didn't I listen to yoga-Pria when I had the chance?

"We can't let things end this way," I say.

"I can."

A voice calls out from inside. "Thom? Is everything okay?"

"Everything is fine, Dad. It's just a canvasser," Thom calls back. Then he turns to face me. "You have to go. Or I'm going to call the police."

There's no point in arguing. I can imagine how this looks. I walk back to my car.

As I drive off, I see Thom watching me from the front window. For a brief moment I think he looks sad to see me go.

20 Making Amends

THE BELL RINGS. A customer has entered the store. I look up from my tablet and see Arshdeep with Pria. Arshdeep looks uneasy to be here, like Pria has a gun to his back.

"This is a surprise," I say. "What brings you two here?"

"Can you get away for a couple of minutes?" Pria asks.

A few minutes later the three of us are sitting

at a metal table in front of the store. "Arshdeep has something to tell you," Pria says.

"What's going on?" I ask.

"Either you tell him, Arshdeep, or I will," Pria warns.

Arshdeep looks at his lap. "I was the one who told Bobby Bentley you're gay."

This was the last thing I expected. Of all the people I thought I could trust, it's Arshdeep.

"Why would you do that?" I ask.

"It wasn't on purpose, I swear," Arshdeep says. "At the party, he asked me if Thom was your boyfriend. I said yes without even thinking."

"I would have made him tell you sooner. But I only just found out myself," Pria says.

I bang my head on the table. I think of all the trouble caused by Arshdeep's slip of the tongue. It's enough for me to never want to talk to him again.

"Thom and I broke up because of what that led to," I say.

"I know," says Arshdeep. "I've felt horrible since

it all went down."

I'm fuming inside. Arshdeep and Pria push their chairs away from the table, afraid I'm going to blow.

Oh my God, I think. My friends are afraid of me. I can't live my life like this.

"It's okay, Arshdeep," I tell him. "It's water under the bridge."

"Really? I would hate you right now if the tables were turned," Arshdeep says.

"Oh, I hate you. But not enough to end our friendship," I say. "I brought this on myself."

"Speaking of which," Pria interrupts. "What the hell were you doing going to Thom's house?"

"I lost my head, okay?" I explain. "My heart is broken. I can't mature overnight. I still have so much growing up to do. I hate it."

"At least you're man enough to admit it," Pria says. "If you hadn't gone there, Arshdeep would have never told me what he did. For what it's worth, your stupid move exposed the truth."

"The truth? Right now my only truth is I don't

have anything. No boyfriend. No wrestling career," I say. "Yay! Everything worked out in the end. Drop the balloons!"

"Don't be stupid," says Pria sharply. "Getting Arshdeep to apologize is not the only thing I'm doing. Tell him, Arshdeep."

"If you come to the School of Hard Knocks with me tonight, I'll try to patch things up between you and Romeo," Arshdeep says.

"Good luck with that," I sigh. "Last time I saw Romeo, he was angrier with me than Thom was."

"But he felt pretty bad for you when I told him you got arrested for punching Thunder."

"Do you think he would listen if I tried to make it up to him?"

"He might. I've never known Romeo to turn his back on a good wrestler. Besides, he needs the talent as much as you need a place to wrestle."

"I'm game if you are," I say.

"Then pick me up after you're done work," Arshdeep says.

I don't think Romeo will let me back into his fed. But it's worth a shot. I know this isn't the answer to all my problems, but it feels like a step in the right direction.

Romeo is horsing around with Troll in the ring when we arrive at the gym. His shoulders go rigid when he sees me standing there with Arshdeep.

"I told you not to come back here, Jorge," he says.

"Don't get mad at him," Arshdeep says. "It was my idea."

"I should kick you both out of here," Romeo says.

"What good would that do anyone?" Arshdeep asks. "Can I talk to you before you go all postal on the guy?"

Romeo throws up his hands and the two of them go into the office. Troll and Brittany hop down off the ring apron to give me a hug.

"How are you, you big fag?" Troll asks.

"Don't you start," I tell him.

"I'm just yanking your chain," he says. "Did you ever find out who outed you?"

I think for a moment. Should I tell them the truth? I think about Arshdeep's words: *What good would that do anyone?*

"No. It's still a total mystery to me," I say.

"Had to be Thunder," Brittany says.

"I might never know for sure," I say.

"We missed having you here," Troll tells me.

Arshdeep and Romeo come back from the office.

"You guys get warmed up for practice," Romeo tells Troll and Brittany. He points his finger at me. "You come with me."

I follow Romeo out the front door. We start to walk around the industrial park. I forgot how much I love coming here.

"So what's this about you getting arrested?" Romeo asks.

"It was so stupid," I say.

"You're telling me it was stupid. Are you trying to throw your life away? Didn't you learn anything while you were here?"

"Of course I did. Things just got so crazy so fast."

"How are your parents taking it?"

"Mom is taking it pretty hard. Dad doesn't say anything. But I can tell he's pretty worried about me."

"So you want to come back here or what?"

"Yeah. I think I do."

"You *think* you do."

"I know I do."

"Ricky will be pissed. This might get you blacklisted."

"I know."

"Screw Ricky. You're still young. You have plenty of time to turn things around. I'll make sure to help you."

"What about my name? What about the gym? I can't just hop back in the ring and expect everyone to forget what happened."

"This isn't my first time to the rodeo, Jorge.

There's a very easy way to work around this. I can't believe none of you idiots hadn't already thought of it."

Romeo digs into his pocket and throws a black piece of fabric at me. I hold it up to look at it. Staring back at me are two eyeholes and two breathing holes. Romeo might be old school, but he knows what he's doing.

21 Masked Man

THE CROWD AT CLOVERDALE is going insane. My match with Arshdeep is getting a great response. In the two months since I came back to Canadian Pacific Wrestling our rivalry has been a big draw.

Arshdeep whips me off the ropes and knees me in the stomach. I go flying over his knee and land flat on my butt. Then Arshdeep tries to pull my mask off my face. Arshdeep gets the mask over my chin but then I pretend to rake him across the eyes. I go for another couple of low blows. He comes back from the beating, but I surprise him with a sucker punch. I pile drive his head into the mat. Then I use my feet on the ropes to ensure the pin.

I take the title belt. I raise my arms in victory as if I actually won the match and it wasn't all planned out.

I have no idea if the marks know it's me under the mask. I don't care. Rumours have swirled in the comments on Bobby Bentley's wrestling blog. I figure that's just Ricky trying to stir the turd.

I make my way back to the dressing area. I try to avoid looking in the direction of the concession stand. Out of the corner of my eye, I've seen Thom watching me a couple of times. This is the first time we've been in the same place since he threatened to call the police on me. I was so worried about what was going through his mind. I'm amazed I didn't screw up the match.

I whip off the mask as I go behind the curtain to towel off. I'm dripping with sweat. I have to wait until the crowd is gone before I can leave, so no one will recognize me. Romeo wants to wait for a little while longer before I show my face again.

"Did you see Thom working at the concession stand?" Arshdeep asks.

"Yeah."

"Aren't you going to say hello?"

"I was thinking about it. But it's been a while. Knowing Thom maybe he's already met someone new."

"I have it on good authority that he hasn't," Arshdeep says.

"Did Pria tell you to say that?"

"Pria would never tell me what to do."

"Pria is always telling you what to do. You're about as subtle as an elephant in the room."

"Would it kill you to say hello to Thom?"

"What if he accuses me of stalking him again? I'm just starting to get my life together. I couldn't handle anyone accusing me of being a psycho. Especially Thom."

"Trust me on this. He's not going to accuse you of being a psycho."

"I'll think about it," I say.

Romeo gives me the signal to leave the dressing area. I poke my head through the curtain to make sure the coast is clear. Then I look in the direction of the concession stand. It's closed down and the window is shuttered.

Oh well. Maybe I'll say hello to Thom the next time we have a show here. I start toward the exit.

"Jorge! Wait up!"

I turn to see Thom coming out of the concession stand. He locks the door behind him and then scurries to catch up with me.

As he gets near, I'm not sure if I should hug or kiss him. There are butterflies in my stomach. I'm afraid to speak because I'm afraid I'll stutter.

"How have you been?" Thom says.

"Good. Better than the last time I saw you." I try to laugh it off. "I never got a chance to say how sorry I am about that. I should have left well enough alone."

"It broke my heart to be so mean to you. I was really confused. I knew you had a lot going on.

But I was worried that if I didn't stop making excuses for your actions, you might really hurt me."

Thom's words are like a shot through my heart. I know he's only being honest. He's not trying to punish me.

"I was pretty screwed up," I admit.

"Pria tells me you've been taking night classes."

"Just high-school math and English. I want to make sure I get my diploma even if I don't go to university. I can't stop hearing your dad's voice, warning me I could get hurt in the ring and left without a career."

"Really? I'm still mad at him for how he treated you that night."

"That night wasn't all bad," I say with an evil grin.

"No. I guess it wasn't."

We leave the arena. There are very few cars in the parking lot. I can see the van in the distance. I don't want to part ways just yet. But I don't know what is left to say. I search my heart for what I've been wanting to tell Thom these last couple of months.

"I know I behaved like a real jerk before we broke up," I tell him.

"You don't need to say that."

"It's true. You deserved better. You treated me like a king, Thom. All people see in me is what I do in the ring. You were the first person who listened to what I had to say. And even if you didn't agree with me, you didn't make me feel like an idiot because of it."

Thom kisses me on the forehead. "And you were the first person I ever went on a date with," he says, "who gave his leftovers to a homeless person. That's the guy I fell in love with. That's the guy I missed when you started doing steroids."

"I gave a homeless guy some food just this morning on my way to the show," I say.

"That's the sexiest thing I've heard in two months."

"There's more where that came from. If you're hungry, I can tell it to you over something to eat."

"I'd like that."

"Let me walk you to your car."

Thom takes my hand and leads me in the direction of his car. He rests his head on my shoulder. It's like we're on our first date again.

Thom squeezes my hand as if to remind me he's still there. The bit of pressure against my palm makes me remember when I'm at my happiest. It's when I'm being true to Thom and the other people I care for. And it's a two-way street. I can't be true to them unless I'm true to myself.

Second chances are hard to come by. I'm not going screw this one up.

Acknowledgements

As always, thanks to my editor Kat Mototsune for all her help and support guiding me through this book. I would also like to thank Jim Lorimer for allowing me to write the books I wish I had access to growing up as a queer teen in the eighties.

Special thanks to Dan Horwood and Wylie Ryan for making sure I got out of the house; Dean Mirau and Chris Dorey for letting me talk my face off after I spent too much time alone; Morgan Brayton for her unwavering support of my work and helping me overcome my fear of public speaking; and Billeh Nickerson for helping me keep it real.